Andrew Lovesey is thirty-four. He is Principal Biochemist at a busy London hospital and is a Fellow of the Royal Institute of Chemistry. *The Half-angels* is his first non-scientific publication. Dr Lovesey is married, has two young children and lives in Kent. His interests include collecting rare cacti and interpreting the Marseilles tarot.

The Half-angels

ANDREW LOVESEY

SPHERE BOOKS LIMITED
30/32 Gray's Inn Road, London WC1X 8JL

First published in Great Britain by Sphere Books Ltd 1975
Copyright © Andrew Lovesey 1975

Set in Intertype Lectura

Printed in Great Britain by
Hazell Watson & Viney Ltd
Aylesbury, Bucks

To Jackie

PROLOGUE

The first evening star shone brightly over the ancient city, casting silver light on the profusion of architecture below, where a multitude of columns and spires reached out into the darkening sky. One building stood as a giant amidst its neighbours, with its feet deep within the city and its summit not far from the gold-edged clouds themselves. For such was the immensity of the Tower of Pandilex, built for the undisputed master of this land. Every day the long, thin shadow of the Tower would slowly creep over the city, and as it did so the citizens would clear from the streets upon its approach, only to reappear when the cheerful sunlight relit the surroundings. The shadow was associated with superstition and was believed to be the instrument whereby all manner of facts were communicated to Pandilex. Small wonder then that he was held in such awe and dread.

At the very apex of the Tower there was a room where the old man dwelt. This was of a cold austere beauty, where the walls were of coloured marble carved in a curious fashion so that those not used to such sights felt ill at ease. Great wooden beams criss-crossed each other in the roof and between these, thick plates were set of a lilac coloured glass to let in light of a peculiar tint from the sky above. White silk curtains embroidered with cabbalistic signs in gold hung at the entrance way. Inside there was sparse decoration, a few tables set with earthenware dishes of fruit and flasks of wine, a couch covered with rare animal furs, and here and there instruments associated with the unusual arts studied by Pandilex.

This night upon the couch the sage was reclining, clothed in a long purple robe stitched with fine silver thread. His age

7

was inestimable. Like a tree of great maturity his skin was gnarled with a multitude of wrinkles and lines. The large bony head was out of proportion compared with the emaciated body. A massive forehead half-concealed deep-set azure blue eyes which even now, despite the present sickness, glittered with a keen intelligence.

Pandilex lay dying, but still Serainis did not come. Despite all the intensive searches and the numerous messages left in prominent places, no word of hope came. To Pandilex it seemed that the final agonies of his body were as nothing compared with the writhing torment of his mind. Only she could answer the question that probed inside him like a caged animal trying to find a way to freedom. What had happened to her? From the moment that Syndra had been put to death in a manner so dreadful that none dared speak of it, Serainis had vanished without trace. Not a word, no sign, nothing left behind. She might never have existed for all that the search parties could extract. Yet surely if she were still alive some word must have reached her by now. Why then did this utter silence greet him unless she were dead? The nagging inside him returned with full dread. Surely he of all people would have known the very moment of her decease, and if Serainis were still alive then there was only one correct interpretation of her present withdrawal. In that case Syndra's fate awaited her. The old man's face twisted in torment as the possibilities went through his mind again. He propped himself up on one withered arm and reached for the copper chalice at the side of his couch. The aromatic liquid gave small relief this time and he knew that soon the death trumpets would be sounded for him. There was no more time for conjecture. He rang the little silver bell and put it back on the marble table.

Raitis, his pupil, came in at once through the curtained entrance and waited silently in front of the dying man. Pandilex, in turn, regarded the other man critically with those curious piercing eyes which had caused numerous people to shudder in the past for fear of the judgement to come. Raitis would rule upon his death, but for how long? Despite the young man's abilities in the arts of which Pandilex was the Master, yet there was something lacking in the finished product of his teachings. Perhaps this deficit would prove to be his undoing. If there had been more time left he could have eliminated the fault and been sure of a continuation of his ideals. It was too late now. The last task would therefore have to be carried out. This, the most important deed of all, had to be left to the last possible moment, in case Serainis returned with remorse and explanation.

'Take this key, Raitis, and unlock the smallest chest standing at the base of the statue of Heraphies.'

The old man unclipped a tiny key from a ring of gold adorning his arm and lay gratefully back on to the pile of furs. His blue eyes followed Raitis as he went over and selected a small wooden box deeply engraved with mythical figures. The box was placed in Pandilex's bony hands.

'That is all for the while. Let no one disturb me until a full hour has passed. I would speak with you then for the last time.'

Raitis looked keenly at his superior and seeing the look of death so evident, hesitated.

'Go,' said the old man sternly, 'do not break the rule of silence now. Have I taught you so badly that you no longer heed my instructions? When you see me next the inheritance of all my arts will then be realised, for in that hour I shall also perish. Go then and leave me for a while.'

The young man bent his head and left as silently as he had entered.

Pandilex took the key and having unlocked the chest, withdrew from inside the container the result of many hours of intensive work. This was to be the final insurance should his hopes regarding Serainis be in error. He slowly and painfully

9

raised himself up with the aid of a metal staff and stood at last still holding with the other hand the contents of the chest. Suddenly a spasm of pain shot through him and he tottered back momentarily. When he had recovered himself he concentrated all his will to begin the task. A monotone chant of words echoed between the marble walls in the room. At a spot some five or six paces in front of Pandilex the air became disturbed, and the robe he was wearing flapped back as a rush of wind gusted past. A void slowly formed in the shape of a vortex rising from the floor. When this had stabilised, an icy voice in the mind of the sorcerer demanded sharply why the forbidden void had been opened. He spoke aloud in humble tones to the guardian inquisitor.

'Oh, terrible Konus, the hour of my death is nigh. Much has been done in this life of mine, the evil of which many bear witness to. Still, because all terms in life are judged on merits relatively based, who knows whether the evil denounced by one man is not the good approved by another? Even before a mirror-glass man perceives not the image of himself as seen by others. The natural law is for evil to be counter-balanced by good, total dominance for one or the other being forbidden. If in this globe there exists a force which by its very nature could destroy this ordained equilibrium, then the natural state would be replaced by a totality of horror unbelievable in its extremes. That such a force is possible I do not doubt, since many saw and experienced to their cost the manifestation expressed in Syndra. With her death such evil should have ceased to be, but the very confirmation that I seek is banned from me. As penance for my part in her creation there now exists a mental block which impedes all attempts to pierce the future. Yet all the cunning of my arts intuitively senses that when I am dead some other will come of greater power to rule this land. Fate leaves my mind in ignorance as to whether such a future will be desirable or not, but before I die I am bound to ensure

10

against this dreadful foreboding. I therefore crave the use of the void.'

He broke off as another bout of pain coursed through his weakening body.

The voice inside returned.

'An answer shall be given.'

He waited racked in pain whilst Death drew nearer from the shadows. Suddenly the assent was given and drawing forth his hand, with a desperate effort of will, he tossed the instrument of his hope into the bottomless void as Death stepped up to take him. There was a rapid flutter of colour as the object went spinning into the shaft there to disappear faster than the speed of light.

When Raitis came in a moment later, only the body of the adept lay on the marble floor. The young man bent down and gazed for a long time at his dead master. Then he turned around and speaking to a guard outside gave the signal for the death-trumpets to be sounded.

CHAPTER ONE

The little Antiquarian Bookshop in Paradise Street had been there for well over forty years. When old Mr Harris had died his son Edward had taken over and respecting his father's literary interests, had caused little change in the business. Some new sections on sport and science had appeared on the shelves, but otherwise the same rows of dusty volumes leant upon each other. Edward was a tall, quiet young man with a dry sense of humour, but since demobilisation after the war had found it difficult to settle down again. Unlike many of his comrades he had not married, although he could make quite an impression with women when he wanted to. They in turn admired his good looks, although more often than not his rather detached manner caused the initial female interest to change to annoyance, when they realised that during their gay chatter his mind had dwelt somewhere else. For the time being it served his own purposes best to potter around in the book shop whilst he tried to get his bearings in the world of business again.

Edward's regular customers were the sort of people who were fascinated by the old books printed generations ago. These collected over a lifetime by Mr Harris senior lay in great profusion everywhere, most being in poor condition with faded print and worn leather bindings. Very occasionally a bargain in resale terms could be found by a determined customer who took the trouble to hunt carefully through the paraphernalia that rose on either side of him almost up to the ceiling itself. Indeed the greatest problem of the business lay in the limited space available inside the shop. To get to the back one had to carefully manoeuvre around the literary obstacle course.

Edward warned his customers half seriously that the further one proceeded from the doorway, the more difficult it was to extricate oneself.

Once the shop had been temporarily closed and cleared of its contents following the discovery by the late Mr Harris that a colony of mice had set up home initially in *Whitaker's Almanack*, and having consumed the facts and figures for 1921, had progressed to greater scholastic heights by nibbling extracts from *The Chancery Laws of England*, digesting *Sunday Sermons* by the Bishop of Winchester, and ruminating upon *Simple Obstetrical Procedures* (by a surgeon of the Charing Cross Hospital). At this point the murine family, having increased twenty fold, represented a serious threat to the business. Their promising literary career suddenly came to the crunch (metaphorically speaking) by the snap decision of the mouse-catcher's dog.

Upon returning the books to the shelves, a number of the oldest books were found to be mildewed and in such a dilapidated state that they had to be thrown away. This created a little space in the shop which Edward's father proceeded to fill with more doubtful 'auction bargains'. On his father's death, Edward found that he had inherited a shop full of decaying books and quite a number of debts.

One day he met a friend in the book business who expressed an interest in acquiring the shop. Edward, in thinking about this, decided that it would be prudent to make some sort of estimate of the stock value. Accordingly he started to prepare a shop inventory of all the books. This depressing occupation took him a considerable time, during which he realised that very little return value could be expected from the books.

Towards the end of this task he found an auction lot inside one of the trunks at the back of the shop, which included a rare first edition of the *Chess Player's Manual* by Steinitz, which improved his humour somewhat. Also of interest was a large, thin volume of considerable age bound with animal hide. An intricate symbol had once adorned the front of the volume, but mould had eaten away the centre part of the design. As Edward carefully opened the book he was interested to see that the interior portion was still in good condition. Each page was covered with thin spidery symbols. At the back of the ancient text there were two unusual illustrations. The first of these was a pattern of closely spaced parallel lines forming geometrical figures of the trapezium and heptagon type. These merged and overlapped together to present a kaleidoscope of symmetry. The longer that Edward stared at the page, the more the pattern appeared to alter, so that lines that formerly receded now thrust forward out of the page. Due no doubt to the multiplicity of parallel lines that encircled each figure it appeared that small points of light danced rapidly between the lines. In fact the whole picture far from being a static thing was a moving, twisting, dynamic illusion. When he looked up from the book he saw the pattern for a few seconds everywhere he directed his gaze.

The other illustration was a lovely work of art executed in the manner of the medieval period. Unfortunately the painting was considerably faded and the detail only showed well in artificial light, which was rather surprising. Holding the book close to the electric light Edward could see that the artist had painted a market scene. A crowd of people in all manner of strange costumes mingled with each other, buying and examining wares for sale or barter. An enormous man stood at the right side of the picture holding the reins of two strong horses whilst he bargained with a pair of soldiers resplendent in yellow and green striped tunics with long swords at their sides. A small circle of women in brightly coloured dresses chatted in a group whilst children played hide-and-seek around them. There were so many people hurrying about and buying from the market that it took Edward some time to appreciate the fine detail of the picture. Despite the women's smiles and the laughter of the children the people's faces were all thin and some of the poorer-dressed looked as if good meals were unknown to them. Beyond the crowds were the tops of some tents and a little further a thick stone wall stretched on either side with soldiers mounted at various points.

Congratulating himself on his find Edward took the ancient volume back to his bachelor flat. After he had eaten the unappetising meal that his landlady Mrs Buckley had left for him, he pushed back the greasy plate and studied the illustrations again, but this time no doubt because he was tired, the details of the picture seemed to merge with the background and the geometrical design played tricks with his eyes, seeming to shimmer with life. He remembered that as a child he had learnt that certain diagrams would produce optical illusions and supposed that this was a more intricate example. Edward closed the book and after stacking the supper dishes in the sink, retired for the night.

However he did not sleep very restfully and his dreams kept returning to the geometrical complex. As he slept he saw flashes of light moving quickly between the lines, backwards and forwards, round and round, whilst whorls of light swung in arcs and crossed each other to disappear and re-emerge further on. Several times Edward awoke with a vision of swirling flashes of light and shuddering lines slowly fading as his consciousness returned to normality. Later he was quite relieved to see that morning had eventually arrived. After breakfast he decided to take the ancient work along to show a friend at the nearby Bonnington Museum of Fine Art.

He had to wait for twenty minutes in one of the galleries devoted to Eastern Manuscripts whilst his friend Mr Crabshawe finished delivering a lecture on the finer points of Etruscan art. At last the talk was over and the friends greeted each other with their usual familiarity.

'So you've found something interesting at last in that shop of yours, have you?'

Tom Crabshawe steered Edward along the passage connecting to the next gallery and they went through into the little office.

'I think you may like this particular bundle,' replied Edward modestly as he unwrapped the parcel that he had been nursing. 'I can't make out the language but then that is not very surprising with my lack of knowledge on antiquities of this age. There are two interesting illustrations at the back besides all the rows of mumbo-jumbo.'

Crabshawe put the book on his desk and switched on a nearby reading lamp. Having made a preliminary examination of the outside of the book, he turned the front cover over. Lines of quaint hieroglyphics stared back at him. Whilst the lecturer poured over the book Edward, to conceal his impatience, walked around regarding the numerous objects awaiting examination that lay on tables in the room. After a while he looked back at his friend whose bald head hovered over the book.

'Well, what do you think of it?' demanded Edward. 'Seen anything like that before?'

The shiny head lifted and Tom stared at him over the top of his spectacles.

'Frankly I'm at a complete loss with this one. As you know I've examined countless manuscripts over the years and quite a lot of unusual stuff has come my way, but this little oddity seems to be in a class by itself. I just haven't seen characters similar to these before. A few of the symbols bear a faint resemblance to the very early Scandinavian cuniforms, but I doubt whether there is a serious connection. As they say, "you pays your money and you takes your choice". For my money I'd say that the most likely explanation is that this represents a personal code used by some person in authority who didn't want his writing read by all and sundry. The difficulty is that without knowing the place of origin the chances of breaking the code are almost non-existent. At the time that this volume was put together there must have been a multitude of regional dialects, whichever country you care to choose. Unfortunately even the experts have only translated a small proportion of these early dialects. Still, don't get discouraged. Let's have a look at these artistic efforts at the back.'

Edward leant over his friend's shoulder and turned the pages to reveal the first illustration. Tom Crabshawe cleaned his spectacles with his handkerchief and pushed them back on to his nose.

'Hmm, now that is interesting to say the least. See how the whole thing changes depending on which way you view it from. A few years ago I put up some wallpaper in our living-room that did the same sort of thing. Half the time you didn't know whether it was the pattern that moved around or the house vibrating. My wife couldn't stand it after a while so in the end I slapped some plain paper over the top. Sorry, old chap, I'm not being of much use today, am I? Let's see the other picture.'

He turned the page over.

'Ah, this is more like it. Not bad at all, although the tints haven't kept too well over the years. Perhaps now we'll have some clue to the source. Mediaeval period presumably, but I'm not sure about the country of origin.'

He tapped the picture lightly.

'This sort of scene could have occurred almost anywhere in Northern Europe. The soldiers probably belonged to a small provincial force and the uniforms tell one little beyond the fact that their master kept them reasonably attired. There are no heraldic devices unfortunately. The rest of the people are a typical bunch for such times, diseased and half-starved most of them. Still at least we don't have to worry about where our next meal is coming from, eh, Edward? How about a spot of liquid lunch across the road?' He closed the book and looked up at the young bookseller. 'I say, are you all right, old chap? You look a bit queer. Here, have a sit down.' He pushed Edward into the chair and fussed around for a glass of water.

'I'm O.K., really I am,' protested Edward feebly, but all the same he couldn't take his eyes from the picture.

The tall man with the two horses on the right of the picture no longer held the reins. Instead one of the two soldiers had taken the bridles, whilst the other stared at a passing woman. At the long wall some soldiers were opening wooden doors and between the gap so formed one could now just perceive a company of travellers approaching in the distance. There was no doubt about it. The picture had changed.

That night Edward dreamt that the network of lines grew in size so that the whole pattern was as big as a house. As he stood before this, the lights between the lines grew more intense and great orbs of brilliance flashed before his eyes. Soon the supporting lines receded and faded until only the twisting chains of light writhed back and forth in perpetual motion. Sometimes a massive ball of fire would appear for an instant and then die away as quickly as it had come. He could not avert his gaze and indeed the whole brilliance of the display had riveted his attention. The whole scene, he numbly realised, was for his attention only, that he was meant to understand something important from the show. He wanted to shout out 'I know, I have found it! This is what you tried to show to me,' but only failure greeted him. He was rejected. The lights grew dim and the dream faded, whereupon he woke up and lay there thinking about the dream and wondering at the intensity of his preoccupation. There was something mesmeric about the way the pattern claimed his attention so easily. Possibly the book work in the shop had proved more exhausting than he had realised and his mind had become over-excited. He got up, made a cup of tea and listened to some music on the radio.

Later when the programme was over he slept again and this time his sleep was peaceful.

He had said nothing to Tom of the changes in the picture and when morning came he began to doubt whether there had been any difference at all. In any case the picture was difficult to see in certain lights. Perhaps he had just not looked carefully enough the first time. In the cold light of the morning the picture yielded none of its secrets, even though he kept the curtains drawn across and held the book close to the electric light. It was apparent that he would have to wait until evening before the inhibiting powers of the daylight had gone. Edward locked the book up in his bedside cabinet and having donned his overcoat, went out of the house. He walked slowly through the streets and avoided the bookshop. The day was spent in coffee shops, a cinema and looking in shop windows, but in spite of this attempted therapy deep inside his brain the lights flashed and the pattern twisted and writhed in an endless dance.

He woke up with a start and found himself in a bus shelter. A woman seated opposite stared down her nose at him with pronounced disapproval. It was late evening now and the stars were out. They glittered slightly and he shivered. The bus was late and full of noisy teenagers. Luckily there was a seat near the back and he sat there, chilled to the bone, trying to ignore the babble of chatter around him. The journey home took an hour and he got back to the flat with a sense of relief. When the electric fire and a meal had restored his feelings he went over to the cabinet, unlocked the drawer and took the book out. The lamp was brought nearer and after a moment of hesitation he turned to the picture page.

A single glance confirmed his fears. The view had altered again. The soldiers and horses on the right of the picture had gone. The market was still there but the customers were different. Also the procession was much nearer now, with some soldiers leading. These had drawn almost level with the doors in the wall. Other people inside the town had drawn forward to meet the travellers.

Edward stared down at the scene. The picture seemed to be alive. The events it represented must be real. This was not an historical recording of an event that had happened centuries ago. It was taking place now just as if the page were a sort of window. Yet the picture appeared to be unmoving. He made a note of the time and rapidly drew a rough sketch of the scene noting particularly positions of the people relative to the stationary objects in the illustration. An hour later he repeated this and was able to detect some movement in the figures. The approaching company was definitely nearer now. The crowd in the market place was turning to see the arrival of the first soldiers through the entrance. A small dog had appeared racing towards the doorway. In the middle of the company there was now visible a wooden cart being hauled by two thin horses. Tied to a rough wooden platform there sat a young woman. She wore a simple dress of green cloth which was splashed in places with the mud thrown up by the horses. Her face was averted but Edward was at once struck by the copper tint of the long braids of hair which swept down to her thin waist. He noticed that the escorting soldiers kept several feet away from the girl's cart. Edward, anxious to see the girl's face, waited patiently for time to pass as events in the picture slowly proceeded. The soldiers took the cart into the centre of the market and led the horses away. Inquisitive at first the crowd were pushed back by the military who took a savage amusement in beating those who ventured too near the cart. As time wore on, the people became less curious and began to disperse. During all this time the young woman had not raised her head. Now as the captain of the escort approached the platform with a flask in his hand, she looked up at her captor and revealed a face striking in its beauty and character. Delicate features were compensated with a determined chin and the most unusual eyes that Edward had ever seen. These were of a mauve shade and were set off by the contrast of the copper-red tresses and wide, thin eyebrows of the same colour. The captain put down the wine flask in front of her so that it was just out of her reach and having enjoyed his little joke, sauntered off.

By now the time was very late but Edward did not dare leave the picture in case the girl had gone when he next had a look. Midnight found him still studying the scene with great interest. Night was falling in the other world of the picture and apart from the occasional soldier passing by, the prisoner was alone. Curiously she was now facing Edward and as he looked at her he thought he detected an expression of apprehension come over her. The time slipped by and his concern for her plight grew stronger all the while.

'Help will come,' he said consolingly. 'I know it will. Don't give up hope.'

Some time later she showed a mixture of intense fear and shock although he could detect nothing in the picture to give cause for alarm. A thought came to him that perhaps she had somehow heard his voice. If so his words would mean nothing to her, just as the language in the book was unintelligible to him. It would be better to keep quiet in case he had frightened her with his well-meant words. If only he could understand her language perhaps he could communicate somehow. He wondered if she in turn could see him but he doubted this. Rather he felt that she might sense his presence from afar by a sort of intuition. She was facing him now but her beautiful eyes looked through him. The properties of the book presumably allowed him a one-way view through the page. Pondering on these possibilities at some length he fell asleep in his chair completely exhausted.

Whilst he slept the only sounds of his world were the murmur of his breathing and the ticking of the clock on the mantelpiece. Now and then a car would go by in the street below, and once footsteps echoed from the paving stones as someone walked past the flat.

In the other world it was also quiet, but unlike the man, the girl remained awake with her own anguished thoughts for company.

'Has madness also come to scourge me,' she said bitterly, 'that in addition to the fate which awaits me, an alien tongue now speaks inside my brain? Truly it is said that the last drops in the cup of life are bitter in extreme.' She shivered slightly and waited for the dawn to come.

As Edward slumbered the now familiar dream returned, but this time the maze of lines had altered in a subtle manner, so that now his attention was directed towards the paths traced out by the moving lights rather than the orbs themselves. Slowly he realised that these fiery streaks formed symbols in the air similar to those written in the book. The more he concentrated the more intense the light trails became. Vaguely he wondered if the shapes were influenced by himself in any way, and as he stared at them the truth of it all suddenly dawned upon him. To prove his theory he tried to empty his mind from other thoughts as much as possible and instead he concentrated upon an image of his own name. The pattern of lights faded momentarily and then a short series of hieroglyphics formed in the space before him. He knew then that this was his name as it appeared in the ancient language, and as this confirmation burst upon his brain, these symbols faded and many others took their place, indicative of his now disturbed thoughts. The excitement of the dream disturbed him and caused him to awake. He hastily turned to the page of the geometrical pattern and saw that the dream was true. Little dots of light traced out the words he thought in the shapes of the book symbols. All he had to do was to think of a suitable series of words and the ancient vocabulary appeared before him. The pattern appeared to be a sort of mental translator. During the next few hours Edward pursued his studies in this direction and managed to obtain a reasonable understanding of the language, having made rapid progress with the aid of the translator device, as he now called the pattern. He wrote out small sentences of the symbols himself and checked them on the mental aid. There was little doubt that in a few days time at this rate he would be fluent.

The clock chimed and he realised guiltily that he had not looked at the window page for some hours. She was still there looking pale and drawn in the morning light. A few people were up and about, including the captain of the soldiers who stood drinking at the entrance to a military tent by the wall. Relieved that nothing much appeared to have happened to her, Edward turned to the beginning of the book and using his newly acquired skills began to read the manuscript.

CHAPTER TWO

'This is the will of Pandilex, sorcerer extraordinary and supreme ruler of the lands pertaining to Elosos, Kant and Tork. Be warned that all who are of faint heart, evil intent or sinister purpose should cease herewith the reading of this book lest the guardians set within it tear one apart, limb from limb, to perish in an agony of pain. For beyond this page are written things which being of a secret and terrible nature, may only be divulged to he who acts as my executor. Therefore cease herewith, or reading on, know that such action implies acceptance of the tasks set forth.

Since in a short while my span of life will close and there is still much to do that time will not allow for me, I have created with no little labour this instrument you now regard, the purpose of which is to enable you to fulfil the tasks that will be forbidden to me. My divinations show that on this globe there exists no one who could undertake such missions as I hope for and bear a chance of success. In consequence this creation has been sent to seek out other places in distant time for one who will return. As the tasks which lie before you may well elicit death in cruel and awesome fashion, to achieve some chance of success it is essential to comprehend fully the history of my past.

There is little point in describing my early days. Suffice it to say that many years ago having been brought up by wise and noble parents, I inherited my father's throne as ruler of these lands upon his death. For some years after this my mother lived on, teaching me how to govern well and also instructing me in the arts of sorcery with which she was familiar. The latter studies proved to be the more exciting and after my mother had succumbed to a fever which not even her arts could cure, I decided to vigorously pursue the quest for knowledge. For a time I travelled widely, learning much from the various adepts that I visited and often exposing myself to great danger in the process, since not all of these sorcerers were of a benign disposition. However, after some years, I concluded that my skills and knowledge now far exceeded all whom I had met in my travels and I returned home to the great city of Jevra, much to the rejoicing of the people. There I have stayed all these many decades, apart from a few excursions from time to time.

After years had passed by in my now sedentary life as a philosopher and administrator of the lands which surrounded Jevra, I began to consider the advisability of marriage in order to continue my family's name after my death. However, the thought of having a wife continually near me and interrupting my critical studies bothered me and so I looked for an alternative.

One day a traveller from the land of Isbos, many miles north of Kant, told me of a curious custom of some of the inhabitants. A local tribe of herdspeople lived high up on the rocky hills adjacent to the slopes of the mountain Evok. Because of a low fertility in the tribeswomen only a fortunate few were able to bear children. In order to maintain the numbers of the tribe at a suitable level, certain selected males took advantage of the services provided by the old ice-witch Vasda. Each time the procedure was the same. The tribesman climbed up to the witch's cave cut deep into the rock near the dead glacier, not far from the mountain top. Having explained his presence, the gifts he had brought with him would be submitted for approval. If all were acceptable, the following night a young virgin of unknown origin would appear at the cave entrance, and in complete silence the two would enter into the dark interior and lie with each other. In due time if the procreation had been blessed fortunately, the ice-witch would send for the man and telling him the name it was to be known by, hand over the infant. Apart from the one first meeting the child's true mother was not seen again, and the tribesman and his wife would bring the child up as if it were the fruit of their own union.

Since by law such things were forbidden within the boundaries of my own lands, the possibilities offered by a visit to the land of Isbos seemed attractive. Providing that a girl of suitable character could be found by the witch, then a union with myself should produce a child of my blood acceptable as an heir to my unchallenged position in the land and to further pursue the studies which were my burning interest.

Accordingly when the snows had begun to melt in the spring I made the necessary arrangements for my absence from the city and set out on the long journey by horse-back to the land of Isbos. Many times on that journey I received omens of bad fortune which should have made me desist from this undertaking, but I was caught up in a fever of excitement, probably due to my leaving the hard mental studies behind in the grey city. I ventured forth out into the green fields and picturesque countryside. Everywhere the colour of thousands of tiny bulbs greeted me. The two suns warmed my face as my horse took me along at an easy pace. It should have been perfect but a number of incidents took place on the way that portended a general conspiracy of evil directed against me.

I rode through a wooded glade where beams of sunlight broke through the leafy shade above. As I breathed in the fresh air and enjoyed the cool breeze on my face, three ruffians dropped from the trees above with daggers poised. My horse reared and saved me as one blade sank into its noble chest. A pair of wiry arms seized me from behind, and as another of the villains thrust forward with his weapon, I uttered aloud certain words of power. They screamed in agony as their hands clawed at their faces. It was dreadful to see them as they rolled over and over on the ground, finding no relief from that which had been set upon them. Within a few moments the last of my would-be murderers shuddered convulsively to his death upon the twisted grass. I spoke the words and recalled that dread thing back to the oblivion it came from. My horse being dead, I was now forced to seek other transport but some hours later managed to purchase a sturdy mare from a woodsman.

The next day having spent a restful night in the woodsman's crude but warm hut, I set off again and by midday had crossed into the border land surrounding Isbos. Here the ground was covered with rosettes of a spiky grass which made progress slow. As I picked my way cautiously around these, I heard a piteous cry ahead and looking up saw a woman tied to a tree, the branches of which drooped over to reach the ground. I hastened towards her and took out my knife to cut the bonds from her, but as I came up to the tree the light altered and no captive stood there. Whilst I stood amazed at this, the branches of the tree which trailed at my feet curled around my legs with considerable strength and started to drag me towards a yawning hole in the trunk. My knowledge regarding defences against such as this was extremely limited and my powers of sorcery had been severely weakened by the previous onslaught. A mighty bough began to press against my chest and terror seized me as I felt my back bending into an unnatural curve. My head filled with a pounding pressure and all went dark as I lost consciousness. For a time I floated in a sea of death, whilst visions of a disturbing nature greeted me. The next I knew I was hearing evil voices, which caused my scalp to crawl with loathing. I opened my eyes and through the gloom saw nightmare forms of green shiny flesh which were travesties of the human form. Worst of all were their heads which were bigger than their bodies and from which layers of curved incisor teeth protruded. They crowded round something on the ground, clawing with long, spindly fingers that moved quickly to their mouths and back again. The place, which no doubt was the interior of the tree, was littered with bones of all shapes and sizes, the nauseating odour being stifling. There was obviously little time to lose. I would have to use all my remaining energy and hope that the consequent drain on my resources would not leave me completely defenceless.

I thought deeply and sent out the commands. On the floor a bone stirred slightly and then another moved. Little by little the scattered remains of all the creatures which like me had fallen into this trap, silently re-formed. A host of ghastly skeletons drew nearer to the tree-people gathered about their prey. A sudden cry from one of them alerted the others and, as they turned their hideous heads, the bony hoard descended with pitiless revenge. Screams of pain and rage filled the murky air. I lay there feeding all my will power to direct the onslaught. Weakness grew over me as more and more energy was taken from me. All at once I found myself sliding across the floor as with a mighty rib-shaking crash the tree toppled over to split open along its trunk. Fresh air rushed in as the wood of the tree groaned and crumbled away. I dragged myself away from the spot where I had been thrown by the impact and after a few yards I fell forward in a deep coma. This must have lasted some considerable time, for when I came to my senses I found that my chin was covered with a long stubble of hair. By now I was without any form of magical defence due to the total loss of psychic energy, which time only would slowly regenerate. The dangers of returning home at this point were greater I estimated than proceeding on to the last stage of the journey, so having located my horse where I had left her, I got on to my mount and travelled on.

A day later the tall majesty of Mount Evok stood before me and I saw a member of the tribe I had heard about. When I asked this young man for directions to the cave of the old woman Vasda, he looked at me queerly and then reluctantly it seemed, pointed out the easiest route up the mountain.

"For a stranger to climb these heights," he said, "it is difficult enough, but to seek out the ice-witch as well is foolishness indeed. Only those familiar with her moods and ways are able to bargain with her and come back unharmed in mind or body. She is old, very old indeed and few are the favours that she grants nowadays."

I thanked him for his advice but nevertheless strode onwards, leaving my horse to graze at the base of the mountain. Initially the path up was easy enough but some hours later the way became hazardous as boulders of rock fell now and then down the slopes and the path was strewn with many small flints. Half-way up I made camp for the night and slept in the shade of a great square rock where some long ferns grew. A cold mist descended rapidly and the atmosphere sparkled with the cold. In the morning I had difficulty in moving my limbs at first and my breath came out in gasps of steam. As I proceeded on my way, the thick lichen on the rocks gave way to a covering of snow and sometime later the great dead glacier came into view. I followed this upwards and wondered at its immense age. Inside the glassy interior were suspended all manner of rocks and plants. At one point I even saw deep within the depths what looked like a man's arm reaching out from below. This produced a sombre mood as I climbed still higher by the side of the great river of ice. Deeper falls of snow covered the ground everywhere now and frosty specks danced in the air. The cold intensified and I regretted that my clothes were not thicker, covered as they were with hoar frost. At last I came to a deep cavern set into the mountain-side and, seeing no one there, shouted aloud, "Ice-witch you have a visitor. Pandilex, ruler of the lands to the South, and Master in the arts of sorcery is here."

My voice echoed from the depths of the cave and then there was silence. A voice in silk tones spoke softly behind me.

"Pandilex is here? The Master of sorcery himself deigns to visit this cold retreat of mine?"

I spun around and there stood before me a young woman in long white robes. Her long yellow hair swept over her shoulders and she stared at me with wide eyes as her scarlet lips curled with a derisive smile.

"Pandilex," she repeated to herself and an amused expression showed. "Pandilex the great adept, seeker of knowledge, who seeking all, knows all. Pandilex, expert in sorcery and therefore invincible, strong in power of mind and body. Surely there can be nothing in the ice-witch's humble powers to attract the attention of Pandilex the supreme."

She laughed and, as the notes of her cry echoed back and forth, I felt a sense of immense power emanating from her. Then for the first time in my life I began to wonder whether what I knew and understood of the magical arts was as much as should have been. From her words she knew how weak I was and how little my abilities were at present compared with hers. My confidence began to go but then a thought occurred and I spoke to her, concealing my uneasiness.

"Pandilex has much to learn from the famed Vasda, witch of the mountain. It is true that I have studied deeply the ways of Power, but also it seems has Vasda, for surely the lovely woman before me belies the years of time that the mountain has known her."

She tossed her head and stretching up her arm snapped off an icicle from a nearby overhanging rock. Her sharp white teeth nipped at the sliver as she considered her reply.

"Pandilex knows well that no spell can arrest Time. Indeed Time it was that arrested Vasda who even now sleeps with her sisters beneath the glacier. I am Kylda who continues the line of ice-witches. That which Vasda did, Kylda does, and somewhat better," she added with a short laugh as she looked with interest at my stern features. "Tell therefore what you seek or depart." Her mouth twitched in a suspicion of a smile. In turn my gaze swept slowly over her and my pulse quickened as I saw how smooth the satin white skin was and how beautiful was the disdainful face with the cynical smile. The icicle cracked as she bit it in two and I thought how exciting it would be to force those cold lips to mine.

"I ask for the service offered by dead Vasda to those who seek the gift of children."

She tilted her pretty head and stepped forward in mock amazement. "What, cannot the great Pandilex achieve the simplest of spells, that which even the lowliest couple can perform? Yet stay," she commanded, as I grew visibly angry at her provocation, "to ask is but enough. I shall not demand the reason though 'tis easy enough to guess. Wait, for I must think awhile." She sat down on a flat rock and after a minute spoke. "What can you offer poor Kylda for the unusual service that you demand?"

From a small leather bag at my belt I drew out the payment. A necklace of rare blue gems flashed in the air.

"These are unmatched anywhere for rarity and beauty," I said. "They are yours in payment for the task."

She looked at them without interest for only a moment and then glanced back at me.

"These have little use for such as I, surrounded as I am by far finer jewels than any woman might wear." She pointed to the brilliant crystal icicles around her and the silver frost upon the blades of grass. "However it will please me to arrange my own reward."

"Whatever you wish," I answered all too eagerly.

She nodded. "So shall it be. Come here tonight when the light grows dim. There is a maiden who will play the part, but being of a higher rank than you may guess, imposes restrictions of secrecy on the proceedings. Therefore she will wear a mask upon her face. You may tamper with this disguise upon peril of your soul, for powers higher than mine will guard her true identity. Neither may you speak one single word to her. However be assured that besides being a maiden of high rank she is also of significant intelligence and beauty. Nor will you find her lacking in desire. Go then and cleanse thyself in the mountain streams in readiness for the night. When you hear the sound of a horn, hasten to this cave and remembering that the rule of silence binds you throughout the night, go with her who awaits your coming. Afterwards having slept, return from whence you came and when the time is right a messenger will summon you to receive that which procreation brings."

She vanished into the cave and I walked slowly down the path. The rest of the day crept by slowly enough and in the evening, having bathed as directed and put on my spare robe I had carried with me, I made my way to within a short distance of the cave and waited there in a great fever of excitement. The air grew colder as night approached and in the distance a murmur of noise from the tribesmen's village at the base of the mountain could be heard. Suddenly I heard the call of a hunting horn from above and had difficulty in keeping my eager approach to a respectable pace.

As I came up to the cave entrance there was no one to be seen and I hesitated, not knowing quite what to do. Then I heard a slight rustle inside and I entered into the gloomy interior. A young woman clad in a robe of white fur stood there with a black mask concealing the upper part of her face. Fine features were evident though and long silky blonde hair trailed down to her waist. Taking my hand lightly she placed her forefinger to her lips reminding me of the need for silence, and advancing into the cave guided me for some time through twisting passages lit every few yards by torches set into the walls. At length we came to a small room decorated with carvings of unknown characters, the floor of which was thickly covered with animal furs.

CHAPTER THREE

'When I awoke in the morning she had gone. I spent much time searching for her but eventually abandoned this useless activity and, having dressed, made my way to the cave entrance. There I remained long enough to eat a small breakfast from some provisions found there and then I started the long journey back to the city of my people.

Upon my return I tried to busy myself with much work whilst the time went slowly by. I kept thinking of the unknown girl and I wondered what her face was like, where she came from, and how the ice-witch had come to hold power over her. As the time for returning to the mountain drew nearer I determined to ask the witch Kylda for answers to these questions.

One day a messenger arrived and left me a missive directing me to return at once. I left in great haste and sped across the country to the land of Isbos. By good fortune no evil attacks happened on my journey and I was soon climbing up the mountain with eager anticipation. In a little while the ice-witch would give to me an heir, and I would question her as to where I could find the child's mother. Surely once I saw her again she would return with me and the child to a happy future together. By now I was at the glacier and as the cave came into view I shouted out with confident expectation "Ho there, witch, it is I, Pandilex, come to claim that which is mine. Appear therefore and conclude your part of the bargain."

From the blackness of the cave the young witch appeared and pointed to the cave. Her mocking voice replied, "I hear you Pandilex the supreme. I trust that my poor services have pleased you well since now you come to claim your own. See now how Fortune smiled upon your greatness and yielded not just one fruitful harvest, but two instead."

She went into the cave and returned bearing with her two female babies of healthy appearance. Looking eagerly at these I was overjoyed despite the fact that no boy child had been born.

"Regard them well," she said. "They bear characteristics of both their noble parents. Truly the blood of their father runs in their veins, for see how the features resemble those belonging to you but in a gentler fashion. Art thou pleased in every way?"

She smiled, but something in her tone irked me so that whilst I should have been at the height of happiness instead I began to worry. It seemed to me that as she stood there silently mocking me, her words had a double meaning which I was unable to grasp.

"Tell me of their mother," I said evasively. "Where can she be found and what is her name?"

Kylda put the infants down and laughed insolently. "So she pleased you mightily, did she, oh illustrious ruler of the South? Know this then that, as before, secrecy prevents my disclosing her identity. However, since she is herself of higher rank than you may guess, I have waived my usual rights in bargains such as this and allowed her to name the infants. Listen well for these are the names they must be known by." She paused and looked meaningfully at me and a premonition of evil crept over me.

"This child shall be known as Syndra and that one shall be called Serainis."

At hearing these words my heart sank. I stepped forward angrily. "These names are such that witches are known by. What trick is this? No witch's blood should mix with mine lest such progeny be of an evil strain. These infants then are from a witch's womb and cannot have been delivered from

36

the maiden that I consorted with. Stop this charade at once and show me now my rightful heir lest I strike you and this evil brood to death with my sword."

In saying these words I drew my sword and lifted it high to enforce my threat, but she drew nearer and putting her cold hand on my sword arm reproached me in silk-like tones.

"Be careful, oh mighty fool, and think well before you kill these infants, for they are indeed yours. Remember now that I promised to exact my own reward for this special task. Well you have amply paid me, though you know not how, and in such currency that will bring forth much interest in the years to come. You asked to see their mother again. Regard well, great adept of all the mysteries. Here is one small enigma which proved beyond your capabilities and which it seems I must solve for you. Your partner in this creative task stands before you. It is I, Kylda, ice-witch of the mountain, whose body you coveted but whose powers you despised. Disdainful lord, who accepted readily enough the delights of an 'innocent maiden', learn this, that despite your elaborate endeavours to provide children of the purest blood, those that will follow you, will bear my blood also. In due time your lands will be ruled by a witch's hand. Such is my reward."

She laughed derisively and the sound of her laughter echoed back from the mountain-side. My head swam with rage and again I lifted the heavy sword.

"Hack away, great Pandilex," she taunted. "Kill the infants that bear your blood. Remember that they are as yet innocent. It is indeed fitting that your greatest accomplishment should be the murder of your own twin daughters."

I turned and stood before her. "This blade is not for them, innocent as they are. It seeks another target," I shouted as I swung the weapon down as quickly as I could. She started to chant a defensive spell but the blade sank deep into her shoulder, and her words ended in a terrible scream as she dropped on to the edge of the glacier. A froth of blood oozed forth from the twisting lips, but even then as she suffered so terribly, her eyes pierced me with an evil curse. I killed her with the next stroke as she lay there in torment, and then as I watched the surface of the blood-covered ice it began to bubble and boil. Slowly the dead body of the witch descended into the depths of the glacier and as it did so she seemed to move as if alive, her dead staring eyes always facing me as if willing some last revenge. Eventually she went deep out of sight in the murky depths, but just as she finally disappeared I imagined that I saw other hands folding over her and pulling her down.

From that time on my peace of mind was disturbed. I returned with the twins to the city and tried to forget the awful look on their mother's dead face, but as the years went by the memory did not fade. The twins grew up into beautiful young women. They were both very gifted intellectually and I soon found that my magical studies advanced rapidly with their help. However a few of the most powerful spells I kept from them, since I had no wish to be outrun in the arts of sorcery whilst I was still active as ruler of the South.

Although born as twins, the sisters were not identical in appearance and whilst Syndra's hair was of a deep brown colour, Serainis had jet black silky hair and her skin was somewhat darker in tint. Similarly their natures differed considerably, for whereas Serainis with all her gentleness had many admirers, Syndra occupied all her time in the magical studies and her manner with all was sharp and uncompromising. In time many noblemen approached me with intentions of marriage to one daughter or the other, but despite my recommendations the girls remained unwed. To me they displayed the correct amount of respect but I think that true affection was lacking. Perhaps this was my fault as I was unable to look at them without seeing some resemblance to their mother, and this sorely affected me. For each other, despite their differences in character, the twins showed obvious affinity and this was a kind of comfort to me that whilst I could not offer them much in the way of fatherly love, they obtained a closer understanding with each other.

The reader of this account may well wonder at the length of this tale. However it is necessary to give detail of these past events in order that full comprehension of my present predicament may be attained. I therefore continue.

After some years I found that my state of health was becoming much impaired due to the onset of a progressive illness which resisted my attempts to cure the malady. One day as I lay weak and ill in the vast tower which was built for my studies of the art of mysteries, I received a warning impulse from that which I had set to watch over the city and its inhabitants. The nature of this thing is best not revealed apart from saying that all news of immediate events within its scan were related to me on a mental basis. This particular warning was so strong that I at once sent out an inquiry as to the source of this evil. Much to my amazement, 'that in the tower' was unable to communicate further after giving a brief but intense feeling of danger within the city walls. The interference with the mental communication clearly indicated that a powerful opposing force was working against me and I therefore sent messengers to summon Syndra and Serainis to aid me in this combat. In a little while Serainis appeared and helped me to fight off a multitude of strong psychic attacks against myself. However these grew more effective as time passed by and my efforts to resist them became much weaker. Becoming desperate, I used a defence of which only I knew the secret and unleashed a force which fed itself on hate and loathing. As the chant was uttered Serainis and I heard a piercing shriek in an adjacent room and rushing through the entrance found Syndra crawling about on the floor gripped in a madness of pain and speaking words which made little sense. Here was clearly the source of the attack upon me. Whilst I arrested the effect of the spell laid upon her, Serainis put her arms about her sister and lifted her up on to a nearby couch. Syndra's powers were completely exhausted and she presented no further threat in terms of sorcery for the present, but I could clearly see that she would have to die before her abilities recovered in full strength. Were it not for her sister's help I doubted whether I would win another such battle. Should Serainis also turn against me then all would be lost. I determined therefore to kill Syndra and decided to execute her in the manner which is usual for assassins in these lands. When I announced my decision Serainis wept and pleaded urgently with me upon her sister's behalf, but Syndra, having recovered he senses, said nothing and only smiled a little when she saw my look.

The special court of judgement gathered the next day at the entrance to the Cave of the Condemned. Here in single file the people with their prisoner walked down the old stone path that wound its way deep into the rock below. Ferns grew in profusion on the shiny walls and from the roof water dripped incessantly. The passage-way ended as the balcony of the Great Cave was reached. Here the people of the court moved round to the circular edge of the rocky projection which extended over a large pit some fifty feet below. Serainis and I took our seats opposite the long wooden winch constructed over the top of the balcony and then Syndra was brought in by the guards and turned around to face me.

"Syndra," I said sternly, "you know the fate that now awaits you in just retaliation for the efforts made by you upon my life. Indeed it has been discovered that many of my closest allies have died from the result of your attack. Those who aligned themselves with you in this conspiracy have already been put to death on my command. Yet even now I am prepared to be merciful with you on account of your sister's plea and the fact that you are my daughter. Tell me then why you directed this conspiracy. Beg this court for clemency in your punishment and perhaps you will yet be spared the journey below."

Syndra turned her eyes to me and in her expression all could read the insolent mockery of her thoughts. Yet she said nothing and stood there disdainful and alone.

"So shall it be. You have set yourself against my authority and the law on such matters is very clear. I condemn you to the pit."

Serainis leaned forward and pulled my arm, begging me to change my mind, but I had already given the signal. Syndra was stripped of all her garments and tied at the wrists and ankles. The rope coiled round the winch was tied to her wrists and she was slowly lowered from the little platform that ran up to the centre point of the winding rod, directly over the pit. The guards slowly unwound the rope and Syndra descended inch by inch, hanging taut, suspended from the rope. The creak of the winch was the only sound for a while as the people above peered down at the slim white body slowly turning at the end of the line.

Her eyes looked upwards all the time, but she said not a word. From the pit below something stirred. A creeping, rustling noise was heard as the great serpent awoke and uncoiled itself. No one knew how old this predator was but for eons of time it had lived there, consuming the unfortunates lowered down from above. Now as Syndra's naked body came nearer, the serpent's evil head rose to meet her. The winch was stopped and she dangled there, as pressing hard against the sides of the pit, the slimy coils sought a grip to enable the horrific head to rise higher. Now the fiery red eyes of the monster were visible as its upper length extended fully. The mouth was a yawning, toothless gap of pink, gelatinous slime. The winch was turned again. Syndra's toes met the serpent's mouth and as she was lowered, so the feet and legs disappeared from sight. Serainis uttered a terrible cry and fled from the assembly. Still Syndra gazed up silently with seething hate. I gave the final signal to the guards and the rope was unwound further. The serpent's neck enlarged, as with a ghastly sucking sound the beautiful white body slid down into the throat. Finally there was a snap as the rope broke below. The court broke into a murmur of excited conversation as I slowly made my way back to the tower. Such was the terrible fate of Syndra.

Despite my attempts to remain impassive in front of the people at the execution, I was much affected by Syndra's death and my state of health suffered a further downward plunge, so that I could see that my life would soon be over. Serainis, whom I wished to question much regarding Syndra's change of attitude towards me, had vanished after the execution. Months after this my efforts to find her place of retreat had failed and I was badly tormented by doubts about her own regard for me. Perhaps she would come back in time, having mourned for her sister and forgiven her father for the necessary action taken. Possibly she had been abducted and was now in peril of her life or even dead. I also had to consider that the death of Syndra had turned Serainis against me and because of such a possibility I took certain precautions for my safety in the short life that lay ahead.

Amongst those who assisted me from time to time in the magical arts was a young man called Raitis whom I selected as worthy to rule after me, should Serainis not return with satisfactory explanation. This man has therefore been instructed as best I can in the short time left, but I fear that he would be no match for Serainis should she set herself against him.

This manuscript thus represents the final precaution that I make to ensure a future of hope for the people of my lands. By mystical enchantment the one who reads this work will be bound irrevocably to the tasks I now set forth. Read on therefore and remember all I have written in these pages.

Seek out Serainis and ascertain as best you may whether

good still exists as an active force in her to counteract the less noble forces inherited from her mother, the ice-witch Kylda. If, as happened with her sister Syndra, the forces of evil have possessed her mind completely, then by any means you have, destroy her without pity. Furthermore there is in my great tower a certain device, which being secret, no one knows of except myself. This you may use once only for protection against an aggressor. Set in the central supporting column of the topmost room in the tower are various carved heads of animals. At the very base there is a mythical bird with six eyes. Press the middle pair of these when danger threatens.

Be warned that all which may appear good may yet hide an evil heart. Those used to the arts of sorcery are expert in the ways of illusion. Therefore trust no one and accept advice only after careful thought as to intentions.

Finally, heed this well. The following words contain instructions for your entry to this world of mine. If you should decide against the tasks set out above, then in a little while you are likely to perish in a manner so terrible that not even I could imagine. Act wisely then and within a day from now complete the preparation for your journey. Wait longer and the fate indicated will greet you, for the hand of Pandilex can strike even after death. Yet tremble not, for should you successfully carry out this mission you will have saved my lands and people from a nightmare future of evil. This will bring its own reward in the harvest of good that follows.

The spells that are set into this book will have sent it far away in time to seek out a man who has, by reasons of his qualities and character, the best chance of accepting these instructions and carrying them out with stealth and guile. It is necessary that protection be given against revelation of your source of origin and the involvement with myself. This can only be ensured by setting barriers in certain parts of your memory, so that those of your world are not in turn threatened if you should fail in your quest. I wish you well. You have little choice, but even so the rewards are potentially great if success is achieved. Should Serainis be intrinsically good, as I hope, then you can do much to help her in the affairs of the South. Follow the instructions now given and may you be of strong and noble heart.'

Edward was fairly open-minded about most things in life, but to believe the contents of the manuscript was asking too much. It was quite interesting in its own way, but he doubted whether the claims to work magic were really more than gross exaggerations on the part of the writer who obviously had a high opinion of himself. Still there was no denying that the moving picture was most unusual indeed and the pattern of lines had certainly led him to translate the language of the book. He turned again to the picture-window, and was startled to see that now there was a crowd of people around the cart, regarding the young woman who stood there, looking at her inquisitor. This was a long, thin woman in a grey dress with crosses embroidered over it. In her right hand she held a sharp needle with which she threatened the girl. Of the eventual outcome of this unequal contest there was no doubt, since a wicker basket just larger than the size of the girl lay near by. Appalled at what he saw, Edward wished there were something that he could do to help. This time he spoke to the girl in the language of the book as words came unexpectedly from his mouth, although he had never heard the ancient language uttered before. It was as if someone else used him to project their own voice. He said to her urgently, 'Help comes. Do not be afraid. I will defend you at all costs.'

Having said this he felt rather foolish as he was not sure how he could help her. Even if he followed the instructions in the book he had no way of knowing whether the scene in the picture was where he would arrive or whether the timing of events there would have changed.

He decided that if he accepted that the girl in the book really existed in flesh and blood somewhere, then he had no alternative but to help her at once. No alternative was right, he thought, for Pandilex had indicated there was no choice unless one wished for a very unpleasant death. It seemed ridiculous that he could take seriously a threat written in a book by someone who must have died centuries ago. Well, there was only one way to find out if the power of the dead magician still worked. He consulted the book and began the preparations. Two large, strong mirrors were required and he managed to purchase these, measuring five by three feet, from a local furnishing store. They were cleaned scrupulously and one of these was then laid in the middle of his room. With an ink marker and a ruler he carefully drew out the diagrams shown in the book on the glass surface and repeated the process on the other mirror. This one was suspended face down some eight feet above the other mirror by fixing the brass chains on the back to the light bracket in the ceiling. Providing that this didn't suddenly give way or the ceiling fall in then the first part was done. He adjusted the bottom mirror until it was exactly in line with the other. Then the writing was consulted again and he tested his memory by writing down the words until all were remembered in the correct order. He stood carefully on the centre of the base mirror and looked at the infinite line of self-reflections extending away from him.

Here goes, he thought, I bet nothing happens and I'll feel a right Charlie, the proud possessor of two unwanted mirrors. He became more serious, concentrated on the words and spoke them aloud slowly. Nothing happened. He gazed at the mirror images and felt annoyed at the deception of the old manuscript. Then, as he looked, one of the images of himself far away behind the others moved, and as it did so he jerked and fell through the mirror, as that which was known as Edward Harris disintegrated into thousands of tiny pieces of light.

A slight breeze from the window disturbed the pages of the ancient volume, as if someone stood there idly scanning the contents. Then the air was still as silence fell upon the room. The book lay open at the picture page but curiously enough this was now completely blank. Later on in the day the sun beamed in through the windows and the pages slowly warped and darkened in the strong rays. Mrs Buckley in her ever vigilant search for rubbish picked up the decaying book and scratched her head.

'What's the good of keeping mildewed stuff like this? He needs his head examined, that young man. Well, he won't miss this one, that's for sure.' She tossed the book in the dustbin and continued her cleaning.

CHAPTER FOUR

The desert was cooling fast as the scorching Arabian sun gradually slipped below the far horizon. As the fiery sky grew darker so the gold-edged streaks above became more beautiful every moment, being highlighted by the sun at their feet. Taylor however was not impressed by such natural grandeur. He had seen it all before, many times over. The sheer predictability of it irritated him. He would have been much more pleased to see some rain clouds about, but they were a rarity in this part of the world. Back in dear old London it would have been a different story. There you could depend on an abundance of what was a unique event here. A sand fly settled on his nose and peered insolently back at him. He swiped at it viciously and the insect flew off in erratic circles.

Taylor swore softly to himself. Why the hell had the bloody corporal decided to go sick on a day like this one? He was the only one who knew the scrub land with any accuracy and the bastard was lying in sick bay, unable to lift a finger let alone act as Taylor's guide. It was all too bad. If he'd had any sense he would have stayed in dreary Aldershot. Having volunteered for an overseas posting, here he was now in a hot, dusty jeep somewhere in the middle of Central Arabia. The CO had been no help either. He'd asked the major for appropriate guidance on receiving his driving orders and obtained the expected reply.

'Local maps of the desert? Good God no, don't have civilised things like that in this forgotten part of the Empire. It's not quite the Chelsea Barracks here, old man. Have to use your bloody initiative you know. I suppose you haven't got a spare smoke on you. No? Oh well, shut the fly screen behind you, there's a good chap.'

The only help had come from one of the locals whom Taylor mistrusted on sight and with good reason as events showed. He had taken the route suggested to him after loading the supplies on to the back of the jeep and had set off as he fondly imagined for Jawad. Three hours later he was now at this spot and no town was within view. A small sand storm was coming his way in the distance so he decided to pack it in for the day and get back to base.

Tuesday night was a good night, for then the local talent came into the camp, ostensibly for the dance but also for other attractions. He swung the jeep around and bumped along the top of the dune. Perhaps that red-headed bird would be there again. Roll on eight o'clock. The locals might be a right lot of scrubbers, but she was definitely high class. This one would require a certain amount of conversational finesse and physical expertise of the sort that Taylor prided himself upon. His fellows came to the point almost immediately. That was where they made the big mistake. A girl like her would need coaxing, just as the patient angler could tickle a trout out of the water.

Steam puffed out of the radiator. The water was boiling in the tank. He stopped the vehicle and lit up a cigarette. Smoke curled lazily upwards in the warm air as he waited for the engine to cool down. Yes, he thought, tonight's session would be good, very good.

Above him the sky sparkled with the light of innumerable stars, but though he did not realise it, he only saw an insignificant part of the cosmos. Somewhere so far away in space that distance from Earth had no meaning, there revolved another planet, the great globe where Pandilex had lived and died.

*

Yola waited for the end to come but the butcher woman was in no hurry to end what was to her a most enjoyable event. Appointed as local official executioner of those mentioned in the lists as public enemies, she reacted as an actor does to the crowd, seeking to exact the utmost terror from her victims. This one, despite her youth, appeared to be a hard nut to crack, but beneath that pale, pretty face the fear lurked, needing only the right stimulus to come shrieking to the surface. Even now the young girl's self-control was wavering on the edge of hysteria at the threat of what the needle could do. Yola strained to speak a protecting incantation but each time she tried, the words were sucked up instantly by some unknown power. The numbing weakness in her mind must be due to this effect and it was now just a matter of minutes before her self-enforced composure would shatter to reveal her terrified feelings to the sneering crowd.

Suddenly a voice of thunder rumbled in her mind.

'Help comes. Do not be afraid. I will defend you at all costs.'

Her mind reeled from this explosive, psychic impact. What was this? The same voice that had entered her brain some time ago had used a foreign tongue then. Perhaps all was not lost. At the moment she was powerless, stripped of all defence by the forces that sapped her will, but the butcher woman did not yet know that. Play for more time and perhaps this proffered help would come somehow.

'Listen to me, you vile creature of torment,' Yola began.

Her inquisitor looked momentarily surprised.

'So you speak now, my pretty dove, do you? We shall soon hear how you sing as well my dear. Perhaps you shall dance for us also.' The woman cackled with laughter and pricked Yola with the needle.

Yola bit her lip in anguish and replied in stressed tones, 'You have gone far enough, woman. I warn you all that I shall set a spell the like of which you have not seen before. There

49

shall come an unknown devil in vengeance upon my behalf and those who are my enemies shall then wish they were safely dead. Even this very instant it speeds to do my bidding. Go from this place before it is too late.'

At these vehement words the small crowd began to talk with each other in some consternation, but the butcher woman silenced them.

'Believe not the words of this little dove. Her wings are clipped very neatly I assure you all. If she had any powers remaining she would have used them long before this point was reached. See now, how great her defences are when my tiny bobbin pricks her rosy cheek.' Her arm drew out and stabbed through the air at Yola. A small drop of blood beaded forth and dropped down the fair skin. Yola's eyes began to moisten.

All at once in front of her, to everyone's amazement, a long, thin column of light formed. Like a long paper chain, a series of misty, identical images end to end clarified and then coalesced into the shape of a man.

The crowd waited no further for developments, but stampeded in panic as they fought to run away from the devil. Within a few moments the entire market place was practically deserted. The vision stirred and slowly put its arm out to take the bobbin from the tormentor. As he touched her she fainted with fear and fell to the floor of the cart.

His own mind was in a complete daze. What was he doing here in this strange place? He could not even recall where he had come from, or indeed even his own name. Something terrible had just happened. He had lost all sense of his own identity. For a moment he stood there in silence desperately trying to remember who he was. Then he realised the girl was bound. He plucked a small knife from the fallen woman's belt and after a few attempts managed to cut through the bonds.

The young girl regarded him curiously and with some apprehension.

'Who or what are you? I did not summon such as you nor would I have the power to do so, yet you came to my aid. What will you do with me now that you are here?'

It occurred to him that danger existed in this place for both of them. 'There is no time to explain now,' he said evasively. 'The sooner we are away from this area the better for both of us. Which way do you think we ought to go from here?'

She took his hand after a little hesitation and climbed down from the cart. They selected the best pair of horses from a number tied up at one of the now deserted stalls and having mounted, she led the way for both of them. He wished his riding abilities were as good. When was it that he had last ridden? He tried hard to think back but there was nothing. Here he was riding fast away from a market town with no memory going back beyond the time when he saw the girl. She must be a vital clue connecting his past existence with the present, but try as he might, no solution came to him. He must question her closely and perhaps obtain some inkling of his own position.

Yola's long, red hair swept out behind her as the wind rushed past. At last it became evident that now no chase could have found them and when they came to a forest glade they rested awhile.

'Well, wizard,' she said with a smile, 'I thank you for appearing so dramatically at such a time of peril. Perhaps you would be courteous enough to tell me who it is that I have the honour of addressing?' She looked at him inquisitively for his strange clothes bore evidence of his obvious differences from the local inhabitants of these lands. He was considerably taller and stronger built than any man she had seen before.

'I'm sorry,' he apologised. 'I can tell you practically nothing about myself, for I am unable to remember anything prior to when I first saw you. The stupid thing is that even my own name escapes me at the moment. Just how I came to be standing there on the cart I don't know. I was hoping that you could tell me.'

She frowned. 'Why do you mock me, wizard?'

'No, really,' he said earnestly, 'I am speaking the truth. I would like nothing more than to know who I am at this moment.'

She got up from the grass where she had been sitting and looked closely at his eyes. 'You look well enough to me, but perhaps I can in turn help you a little. My own name is Yola though you will not tell me yours. Sometimes I can hear the thoughts of people if I try very hard. Perhaps I could tell you what is hidden from your consciousness. It will take but a little while if you do not resist my attempt.'

He assented eagerly and she placed her cool hands upon his forehead. Some minutes passed as deep in thought she strove to break down the barriers implanted in his mind, then she relaxed and looked perplexedly at him.

'There is a wall beyond which I cannot see.' She looked troubled. 'When I was held prisoner in the market I heard a voice promising help to me, and I longed with all my heart to see a deliverer. Perhaps the force of my will created you by some magical means and yet I scarcely believe this could happen for me, although there are those whose powers may be great enough for such skills. Besides your face bears marks and scars which healed a long time ago and point to a previous existence elsewhere.'

'Maybe my memory will return in time.'

'All is possible, friend. In the meantime I must find a suitable name for you. Yes, I shall call you Jeron, which means a wizard of great skill.'

'Some wizard,' he said, 'who cannot even recall his own name.'

She laughed and placed a hand on his lips. 'What matters a name? You are Jeron now because I have named you so and

Jeron you shall be. A wizard you were undoubtedly in order to appear in the way that you did.' She explained the manner of his appearance and his bewilderment grew. Was he really a maker of spells? Did such people exist? He wasn't at all sure. Perhaps she was right. In the absence of other evidence it was best to accept her advice for the present and not worry too much about the past. All the same just how did one make spells? It was possible he would find that out too.

'What had you done to be a prisoner?' he asked.

Yola raised her eyebrows in amazement. 'Don't you even know the laws in this land of Kant?' He shrugged his shoulders. 'Well then I can see I will have to teach you something of this place. Now let me see. This land has seen much in terms of past history. The pattern has always been the same, an age of peaceful years being followed by strife and famine. Then when all seems lost peace comes again to rule for a while. We are now in a time where the quiet luxury of a previous generation has been disturbed by a more ambitious and less happy age. Things that would have been deemed cruel and inhuman years ago under the golden rule of great Pandilex are now hardly noticed above the commonplace. With the sage's death civil war has swept the lands as those who possess much power seek to crush their rivals. Under such conditions it is wisest by far to speak little and listen much before you declare which way your interests lie. Such was my undoing, for in a moment of weakness I showed that my loyalties did not coincide with the majority and very soon found myself trapped by those who I had deemed to be my friends. Remember deceit is the rule here rather than the exception. You and I may trust each other with our knowledge since my life was saved due to your intervention, and in your peculiar state you have no choice but to accept my advice or you would be quickly lost.

'Now listen carefully. I work for those who would restore the former peaceful state but because of the danger of capture, at present I think it best that no names be divulged to you until we are safely back with them. Therefore trust me in all things except if I am captured, since then torture makes any person vulnerable. We will go to the company of friends, but not by direct route since those who may watch us might guess our ultimate objective and proceed before us. We will spend the day in hiding and move mainly by night, which means we shall soon be riding again. In the meanwhile let us endeavour to restore your own abilities to you, since sorcery of the high potency you first displayed would be of great benefit to our cause.'

They spent some time deep in conversation whilst Yola tried to remind him of the basic elements of magic.

'Few people now have any great talents in such arts, for those that did, warred bitterly on each other to such an extent that most of them died or vanished for all time. Those that were left took good care to banish their weaker rivals, or else kept their knowledge secret. Nowadays, four factions exist in these lands of the South, although doubtless there are others in the lesser known lands. These four continually plot against each other, and their followers infiltrate each others' camps so extensively that no one can now be sure just which camp his fellow traveller really belongs to. Besides my own leader, there is Raitis, who was named as successor to Pandilex, Tokin, the self-styled Regent of the land of Elosos, and Zaduk the Deviant.

'All I can teach you is the type of humble magic which those such as I can manage from time to time. However it may well be that since you are not a native of the South, the magic pertaining to you is of a different kind. Still, this much will I show you. Remember that each time an act of power is performed the person who casts the spell is thereby weakened in proportion to the magnitude of the act. Therefore only those who are expert sorcerers may dare attempt the colossal enchantments that have occurred now and then in the history of these lands. It is often best to counter-attack at the point when one's adversary is weakened from this temporary loss of power. A novice in the arts may well require several days to recover his original strength after a meagre act of sorcery, whereas the truly great adepts may merely pause for a few seconds whilst new energy floods into them. From this alone one can judge the calibre of an opponent. Now let us see whether you can do these simple tests.'

After a little while she had to admit his total lack of response and, as it was becoming dark, they untied the horses and went on their way again in silence as she had instructed. Yola was considerably puzzled by her companion, but felt intuitively that his presence in this game of life and death could well tip the balance in her leader's favour, since there might be little defence against the stranger's magic of unknown source, if only she could help him to remember. Anyway she would certainly do her best. He was quite handsome and it would be no hardship to have his company as they moved towards her headquarters. One thing kept her further apart from him and caused her to adopt some caution. When she had looked into his mind with considerably more power than she had led him to guess, the startling picture she received was not that of some form of amnesia but instead a total blankness. She was shocked that it was not his memory that was malfunctioning, but rather that where his memory should have been, there was nothing, nothing at all. Was he deceiving her? She did not think so. After all she owed her life to his efforts. Yola shook her head and gave up the problem for a while. It was difficult enough trying to perceive the correct way through the dimly lit forest. Animal noises greeted them now and then but they were not troubled by the wild life as they pushed forward with their horses. Soon the vegetation gave way to more open country and after some searching she found a well-trodden path for which she was looking. This led to a small wood on the brow of a hill and here she pointed out a distant collection of spires and high buildings.

'There you see the great city of Jevra, built eons of time ago when civilisation was young and this globe a better place to live in. As the generations died so each ruler of the South raised greater and more magnificent buildings within the city to mark his imprint, but of these monuments none stands more characteristic of the ruler's mental stature than the long spire in the middle, called the Tower of Pandilex.'

At these words Jeron started and felt a thrill of excitement run down his spine. The Tower was important. It meant something to him although the reason was hidden from his thoughts at the moment. Yola noted his agitation and asked him about it. He explained how he felt about the Tower and urgently requested that they proceed in that direction so that he could have a closer look at it. She was not very keen on the idea but when he persisted she gave in.

'The city is under the rule of Raitis who has an alliance with Tokin. I have not heard many ill things said of Raitis, but to fall into the hands of Tokin would be a terrible fate. If go we must to the great city then I shall have to obtain some less conspicuous apparel for you, otherwise your journey will be ended quicker than you realise. I have some friends in the northern part of the city who will provide the necessary garments. When we get within a short distance of the city walls I will proceed alone and return with the clothes later.'

They continued their journey and did as Yola directed when they were nearer the great granite walls which effectively hid most of the lower buildings from their sight. He settled down for a long wait on the top of a small hill and towards the end of the day Yola came back with clothing which fitted him surprisingly well. There was also a type of chain mail shirt and a short but sturdy sword. Jeron found the latter somewhat heavy to hold but tucked it into the leather scabbard at the side of his belt. Yola had enveloped herself in a long, grey cloak which prevented anyone from seeing her face in detail. After eating the food she had brought with her, they advanced to the city gates and despite his acute worries, passed the guards without query. In a short while they stood before the huge Tower of Pandilex, the summit of which faded out of sight amongst low flying clouds. Jeron became tense as he sensed a pull of his body towards the entrance to the Tower.

'What is the matter?' asked Yola urgently as she noticed his efforts to counteract the pull. He told her of the effect upon his will and she grew troubled.

'The Tower has strange properties and may well influence people against their wishes. Perhaps the attraction for the Tower that you initially displayed was caused to trap you.'

'I can do nothing to stop it, Yola. Stay there, for if this is some kind of mental trap at least you shall not be caught along with me.'

The force which pulled him towards the entrance now proved irresistible and he left Yola very worried as his legs carried him towards the building. She had enough sense to see that intervention by herself would achieve nothing, and concluded that the best thing to do was to quietly wait outside and hope that her presence would not be especially noticeable amongst the few people passing by at that late hour.

There were no guards at the doors as Jeron walked quickly through. Inside there was a small, circular room with many doors. Which one of these should he go through? His legs seemed in no doubt at all as he went to a small door on the right hand side.

CHAPTER FIVE

The sandstorm was worse than he had expected. Taylor crouched behind the windscreen, holding his arms over his head as if he were a monkey at a zoo. Some bloody monkey, he thought. I'll have a few kind words to say to that friendly, smiling Arab when I return to base. He wrinkled his nose as the grit found its way into his clothes. There seemed to be no let up in the ferocity of the blast although the wind changed direction every now and then.

Most sandstorms were relatively mild affairs, so Oakley had told him once. Sit tight, keep your mouth shut and preferably your eyes as well and contemplate your ruddy navel, hoping that the sand about you rose no higher than your neck. Only a few storms were 'big fellers', likely to cause death and destruction. Taylor wondered whether this one qualified as a 'big feller'. Whatever the species, it was keeping him from moving homeward and that was quite unforgivable since it was Tuesday. He wouldn't make the first dance now, that was for sure. He thought of the red-head. A couple of quick shuffles round the floor, then a furtive 'Isn't it hot in here? Let's go outside for a bit'. For a bit all right, oh yes. His skin reddened as the sand particles lashed against his face, stinging him. He bent down further inside the jeep and tried to dismiss from his mind the holocaust going on outside.

He'd first seen her two dances ago but had joined in the general rush towards her too late to make any progress. Standing with the other wallflowers at the back of the hall, he eyed her gliding round the floor in company with Sergeant Pyke of the flat feet and fishy eyes. She moved in a sensual way, her bottom wriggling erotically as the beat music hotted up. By the time she left the hall with a perspiring and exhausted Pyke in tow all the single men were having fantasies about her.

The next night had been an equal success. Someone had the bright idea of requesting an excuse-me. She was tossed from one eager male to the next in a fervour of masculine excitement. No dancing was done but a number of holds were tried. Finally the colonel restored the atmosphere back to Victoriana by insisting on a St Bernard's waltz, and limped alone around the floor with his lady whilst everyone else made for the bar. Taylor didn't see her after that. He smiled wryly as the sand bit into his hair and the wind screamed madly about him. The centre of the storm was fast approaching and the whole desert area around the isolated jeep became alive as the sand dunes shifted and changed in shape.

There was a twisting staircase on the other side of the door and Jeron ascended this cautiously, trying to slow down the movement of his feet. This spiral staircase went up through the floorboards of the rooms on each level so that he could see the interiors as his climb progressed. His footsteps echoed hollowly as he went higher and higher, but he met no one. Rooms filled with manuscripts, statues of weird beasts, armour, instruments of astrology and other paraphernalia passed him on his way upwards. From time to time slit windows cut deeply into the thick walls showed him his present height. He tried to rest awhile on the stairs to get his breath back, but the pull on his body was relentless. Up he went until he turned around another twist in the stairs to come up abruptly against a thick wooden door. Carved upon the wood were the words 'Enter and be judged, for the Guardians will know thee'. These words for some unknown reason struck a chill in his heart, but the force which had driven him here pushed him on and he opened the heavy door slowly, and went through.

The steps led upwards again but he noticed that they were suspended over a deep shaft which presumably led down to the street level. Some distance above him the stairs led to the next room. As he went up the handrails stopped and he relied on his feet to maintain a balance. When he looked down to see where the next step was he was shocked to see that the entire flight of stairs had vanished. He was standing suspended over the deep shaft without any visible support at all. At once his balance was disturbed and he began swaying from side to side.

A few feet away a woman in white robes appeared and held out her hand to support him. Jeron instinctively moved his body to catch her extended arm, but the pull on his feet kept them glued to their position and he quickly realised that movement towards the woman would have meant his death by stepping out into space. The vision faded and then a man came forward from the darkness on his left, holding out a stick just out of reach. Jeron ignored this and lowered himself down slowly, feeling for the invisible steps that supported his weight. Gradually he moved forward using his sense of touch until at last he drew himself up to the room above.

Here there were no more ascending steps and presumably this was the highest level within the Tower. The room where he stood was very small and there appeared to be no exit, apart from the staircase by which he had come. Indeed Jeron felt rather disappointed that his long climb had terminated in such mediocre surroundings, for the room was box-like and there were no windows to look out upon the city. There was nothing to be gained here. Then a calm voice spoke into the air around him.

'Having come thus far, come a little further, into the presence of Raitis, ruler of Kant, whose home this Tower is. Only if you have evil intent need you fear my wrath. Enter therefore and be judged according to your merits.'

A section of the wall opposite fell away and through the hole

60

so formed a much larger room was revealed. Jeron walked hesitantly through the space and found himself standing inside a richly decorated room where the walls were covered with fine tapestry and silk curtains, and an abundance of beautiful furniture greeted the eye. Tall wooden columns supported the ceiling and were curiously carved with strange beasts. Coloured glass panes set into the ceiling let in light of a pale lilac shade. Seated on a couch was a tall, thin man with a dark beard and sunken eyes. Raitis beckoned Jeron to come nearer.

'Greetings, my visitor, who knowing how to mount my staircase has thus gained audience with me. Tell me then your title as I have told you mine and since no man unacquainted with magic would have come this far, I would know your purpose also.'

Jeron thought quickly. 'I am called by some Jeron, having no other title worthy of mention, and since I come from lands far away I wished to see how the great city of Jevra appeared from the dizzy heights of the tallest building, for the Tower of Pandilex is mentioned by many travellers from afar.'

Raitis regarded him coldly. 'I will forgive your error since your insult was tempered with ignorance. The sage Pandilex is long since dead and the building in which we converse is the Tower of Raitis if it belongs to anyone. However there are many in the city who would say that the Tower belongs to no man but exerts its own power and will. They are fools. It is but an extravagant creation of architecture designed by a warped mind intent upon impressing the ignorant.'

Raitis looked at his visitor with keen eyes for several minutes until Jeron began to feel decidely uneasy, since he realised that as with Yola, so Raitis was delving into his thoughts with a piercing intensity. There was an increasing feeling of pressure within his head and then suddenly it ceased.

'Well, friend Jeron, it seems that you remain something of a mystery, for only partial truth can be read within your mind.

You have set a barrier beyond which not even my efforts can get through. There is an alternative though, which you may not have considered. We shall receive your shy companion who waits so patiently outside. Perhaps I can persuade her to be rather more forthcoming.' He spoke certain strange words with emphasis and another section of the walls opened to admit Yola who seemed to be in a trance, much to Jeron's surprise. She ignored him and walked straight up to Raitis to allow the adept to penetrate her mind without resistance. Anger visibly crossed the man's face as he realised exactly where her loyalties were. In turn frustration grew when he found that she knew as little as he did concerning Jeron. Turning to him he said, 'This woman is a self-confessed opponent of my rule, being a follower of she who is named Serainis. Also you have kept your true identity secret from me. I see no reason why I should spare your lives, coming to me as you have in deceit. You will die now as many have before you, who thought to cause me evil.'

He turned upon his heel and walked swiftly towards a bell-rope. The name Serainis had had an electrifying effect upon Jeron, who as he looked about in alarm, saw a curious carving at the foot of the main supporting roof column. At once he knew that for some unknown reason his only hope for Yola and himself was connected with the strange six-eyed beast. Raitis pulled the bell-rope for his soldiers as Jeron ran quickly forward and placed his hand upon the carving. A trap door burst open and he fell back in fright, as from the dark interior something large and feathered flapped out. Almost the height of a man it stood, with blood-red plumage and wicked, cunning eyes which darted evil glances at the three humans petrified with fear. The long, razor-sharp beak opened to reveal rows of pointed, yellow teeth. Great scaly feet terminated in hooked talons thicker than a man's finger. With a screech it scrabbled across the floor and sank its claws deep into the chest of Raitis who screamed terribly. The feathered monster drew back its awful head with slow deliberation and drove the great hooked beak savagely forward into the face of the sorcerer. There was a sickening crunch of splintering bone as Raitis's skull burst open. Paralysed with terror Jeron and Yola watched the body fall to the ground. Then the figure of the bird twisted unnaturally and its shape changed hideously for an instant as it folded in upon itself, and so collapsing, vanished into the mutilated corpse of Raitis.

Footsteps sounded coming from below. Yola recovered first and dragged Jeron with her over to a small square flap in one of the walls. Lifting this she showed him that it was an exit chute, and sitting on the edge of the tunnel, pushed herself off and away. He followed her as quickly as possible and heard the people entering the room as the trap door flapped shut behind him. Faster and faster they slid along, round and round, until suddenly the speed slowed as the chute became horizontal. They picked themselves up from where they had fallen and looked at the surroundings. They seemed to be underground judging from the dampness of the walls. Yola found a door in a corner and they climbed up some stairs to find themselves at ground level. They cautiously left the Tower, but no one made any comment as they hurriedly walked away along the city streets.

Yola touched his arm lightly. 'We must get out of the city before the soldiers and spies of Raitis detect us. However, my friends here are also in danger now, since Raitis having read my mind would have known about them and perhaps had time to inform his spies by telepathic communication. We must therefore warn them to flee from Jevra before we leave.'

She pulled him back into the gloom of a side-passage as some soldiers marched past. When they had gone the two of them continued their route into the back streets of the city.

'Tell me,' she asked curiously, 'if you are not a wizard then how is it that you raised up that dreadful creature against Raitis?'

He anxiously tried to impress upon her that he thought he was no great magician, but his explanation sounded weak even to himself. The name Serainis which Raitis had mentioned had galvanised him into action and caused the horror to be released. Who was Serainis? He asked Yola, who told him about the legend of Pandilex and the ice-witch.

'It is not certain how much of the story is true, and how much has been magnified out of proportion with repetitive telling of the tale.' She guided him along a narrow lane which was badly lit. He wondered if Serainis held the true explanation of his present plight. Raitis had exposed Yola's secret that she belonged to the camp of Serainis, so presumably they would eventually proceed to meet up with her somewhere.

His thoughts were interrupted as Yola stopped outside a house in the cobbled street and knocked on the door according to a set pattern. A very tall young man opened the door and upon seeing Yola gave a pleased chuckle and welcomed them inside.

'His name is Evran,' she whispered, 'and a good comrade to have on one's side. His wife was killed by Tokin's men and since then a small army of the Regent's soldiers have felt Evran's sword. He is inclined to be a little hasty in decisions but nevertheless is a very valuable friend.'

Two other people in the room were introduced to Jeron as Ginah and Tiros. The girl was young and had a pale, thin face as if she had suffered much in the past. Her companion was thick-set and wore many battle scars. Despite this his eyes twinkled with amusement from time to time and Jeron soon found him to be a likable fellow. Once the purpose of their meeting was explained they all agreed to leave at once for the camp of Serainis, rather than wait for arrest by the followers of dead Raitis. Whilst the others made their arrangements,

Jeron and Tiros went out and purchased five strong horses for the long journey ahead. Not many soldiers were about, but as Tiros explained, most arrests followed discoveries by informers rather than the army. When they got back the others were ready and they set off without delay. There were so many other people on horseback in the city even at that late hour that the group of five was not particularly noticeable. They stopped once just inside the city walls to obtain provisions for the journey and then left for the countryside without hindrance.

It was two days later when they were riding through uneven terrain, where there were many small hills and slopes to negotiate, that Jeron began to feel that they were being watched. No visible evidence presented itself but as they journeyed on and the feeling grew stronger, he spoke anxiously of this to Yola, who showed no surprise.

'Indeed my friend we have been followed and spied upon for some time now, but whilst those who watch are in smaller number than us, we have little to fear from them. Only if others of their kind join in force will we need to look to our swords.' She patted her hip and he was amazed to see that she too wore a small sword. No doubt she was better at using it than he was his weapon, he reflected. Why was it that such arms were so unfamiliar to him? His own lands must be very far away to account for the strange feelings with which he viewed everything here. His red-headed companion interrupted his thoughts again with her pleasant voice.

'Those that followed us have given up now. We shall have no trouble from them after all.'

'How can you tell when they were never visible to us?' asked Jeron perplexedly. She laughed at him.

'Why of course by the same method that you used to detect them. Only it appears that my mind has a sharper sense than yours, as is to be expected since intuition has never been scorned by women. There are some such as Serainis who have developed this gift to a remarkable degree. Even now no doubt she knows of our coming. Tokin's spies have little chance of penetrating her abode and those that have tried to do so have not returned to their own camps. Bear this in mind, Jeron. Keep nothing from her for she will detect your unsaid thought as though your lips had shouted it. Do not look so worried though. I am sure that she will like my good friend Jeron even if he is still somewhat of a mystery.' She leaned forward in the saddle and touched his hand for a fleeting moment, and this slight action made his cares and worries vanish completely, as if she had cast a spell upon him. Perhaps she had. He suddenly wished that the others were not so near. She tilted her head slightly and seeing the admiration on his face, smiled a little and gazed ahead. His rather obvious manner contrasted strongly with the sophisticated ways of Serainis's courtiers.

Towards evening they came to the Quartz Castle where Serainis and her followers lived. After initial challenges by the guards, they went over the long drawbridge and came up to the gigantic keep. The castle was in fact a solid extension of the rocky hill on which it stood, and the keep had been hollowed out of the sheer quartz mound at the top. Due to the optical properties of the mineral the visual effect was startling, particularly when, as now, sunset approached. A wonderful, crystal castle, thought Jeron as he dismounted and watched the horses being led away. Tiros was signalling good-naturedly to him to hurry up and enter the keep. The five of them climbed up a long staircase and were ushered into a large courtroom. There were many people gathered there in gaily coloured clothes, chatting to each other, but as the dusty travellers entered silence fell for a moment. Then above them a woman's voice spoke in cold tones.

'Welcome back, my faithful ones, who have served me well

beyond these lands. I see once again Yola and Ginah prettier than ever, Evran of the warlike spirit, and Tiros of the ready smile, but who is this tall friend of yours who stands so aloof?'

Serainis sat upon a balcony throne and looked down upon them. Without any doubt she was the most beautiful woman Jeron had ever set eyes upon. Fine delicate features contrasted with sensual ruby lips, and long, jet-black hair which cascaded down her violet robes of office. A small gold chain was wound around her neck and was the only jewellery, but above all else the onlooker's attention was transfixed by her startling green eyes. These glittered like brilliant emeralds and were highlighted by long, thin eyebrows which swept upwards.

Yola replied with deference. 'My lady Serainis, this man is he whom I have named Jeron, since his true name has not yet been revealed to me. By his magical intervention I was rescued from those of Tokin's forces, and as doubtless you know the lord Raitis, having captured us, died in terrible manner from a monster conjured up by Jeron. Thus am I doubly in debt for recovery of my life to this man, who commanding such powers, I have so aptly named.'

Jeron looked at Serainis with interest and his pulse increased rapidly. He hoped he didn't look as nervous as he felt, and tried to assume a nonchalant expression, but ended up feeling rather foolish. Suddenly, without warning, he felt his mind being explored by something much more powerful than he had felt with Raitis or Yola. Blood drained from his face with the effort to withstand the enormous pressure within his mind. It ceased quickly and he guessed that Serainis had absorbed all his recorded thoughts and memories since he had first seen Yola. He felt annoyed at this invasion of his privacy. Even his secret admiration for Yola had been noted, he supposed. Yola was right. No one could keep a secret in the company of Serainis. The points of green fire bore into his eyes again, and she spoke in cold tones which held a hint of mockery.

'We bid you welcome and thank you for your services to our cause. With Yola lost we would have been considerably poorer in power and spirit. When you have rested from your long journey we shall talk further and see in what manner we may repay you.' The blood-red lips smiled at him and he felt enthralled. Be careful, he thought, I must be cautious in my replies until I know these people better.

'Thank you, my lady,' he answered, 'but I require no reward for what took place, since I am content to see Yola alive and well.'

Serainis raised her eyebrows a little and looked at Yola who was more than a trifle embarrassed by the sudden attention of all the court. One of the noblemen in the crowded room said something in a loud whisper to his compatriots, and they all looked at Jeron and laughed. He felt annoyed and foolish in the presence of this proud gathering and wished his words had been better chosen. Serainis beckoned Ginah to speak with her up on the balcony, and the silence lapsed as general chatter took over amongst the courtiers. A number of them came over to his companions and greeted them as old friends. In the midst of this activity Jeron stood alone, and heartily wished that he was elsewhere. It was obvious that his past life hadn't been spent idly gossiping in a court. His new friends were happy to be back here, but this was not his home, and if it had not been for Yola he would have left as soon as possible. She spoke behind him.

'Oh dear, what a long face my strange magician has this evening! I think perhaps this gay company does not agree with him.' She smiled consolingly. 'Never mind these people and their ways, for their curiosity will last but a short while and when they know you better as I do, they will cease to be such prying strangers. Now this time, for a change, I will rescue you.

Come with me and I will show you more of this unique castle.'

They left the hall to his relief, and walked through various apartments, Yola explaining the purposes of the rooms to him. When they were leaving a small library he stopped her, and taking her hand gently, drew her closer.

'Yola,' he began earnestly, 'as you have seen I am very clumsy with my words. Nevertheless what I said was true. You must know if you can read my mind the thoughts I have about you.' He stopped because she had quickly put her hand upon his lips, and whispered to him in urgent tones. 'Caution, Jeron. One may rarely speak in this place without being overheard. I know what is in your mind as you say, nor do I have to use my psychic powers to see it. This is not the time or place to pursue such a conversation, for only when we are truly alone may we share our most secret thoughts.' She looked at his downcast face and laughed a little. 'Be not so dismayed, sad magician. You are still my good friend and will remain so.' Her lovely face had moved closer to his and the long coppery hair brushed over his cheeks. Then too soon it was over and she was walking on to the next part of the castle.

CHAPTER SIX

Taylor woke up and stared about him. The jeep was almost buried in the dust. He got out of his seat and stood on the sand. His watch was still going, so at least the grit hadn't entered into the mechanism. It was far too late for the dance night now. He cursed and swept the sand off the jeep bonnet with the back of his arm, the hot metal singeing the hair on his skin. He felt inside the vehicle for an oil rag and used it to wipe away the rest of the sand from the machine. With great effort and a lot of perspiration he made a pathway in front of the jeep, pushing away the sand that had mounted up against the wheels, and then started up the engine. It coughed and died on him. Inside the bonnet he discovered a whole beach of sand. It took him a good hour before he was satisfied that most of the dirt was cleared out, and the motor was in working condition again. He finished the last of his liquid refreshment, and threw the cola tin over his shoulder. The motor started this time and he drove the jeep slowly up and over the edge of the dune, looking for a landmark to get his bearings.

With a shock he realised that the whole contour of the desert had changed. A series of great ridges lay before him hiding the horizon from his sight. He swung the jeep round and drove for a little while up and down, over and under, as each dune rose to meet his approach. It was hopeless trying to rely on landmarks. In theory he should have seen the radio mast at Jawad, but each rise of sand before him blocked his view. He estimated a course based on the position of the evening sun and hoped that when he eventually left the desert behind his camp would not be too far away. The air was still very hot although the sun had lost most of its power by now and lay glowing low in the sky behind him. There would be some caustic comments when he arrived back so late this time, still carrying the undelivered supplies of office stationery. Foster would have it in for him undoubtedly. 'Went for a little ride in the desert, did you? Turned back because it got a bit breezy, eh?'

'Oh, piss off, Foster, what's it to you anyway. Why don't you try driving in the sandy sunshine yourself for a change, instead of staring at Molly's backside all day long in the office.'

The jeep careered along on an endless switchback, sometimes stopping as the front wheels sank into a soft area, whereupon Taylor, cursing, would get out and wearily push the vehicle back on to firmer ground. He lost count of the time as the dunes seemed to get higher and higher, instead of flattening out as he had hoped. The sandstorm must have been worse than he had thought. The sun was low down on the horizon but there was still enough light to judge his direction from. He felt tired and hoped that the journey would soon be over. If all had gone right with his calculations he should be fairly close to the camp. He stared ahead of him but could see no mast scaffolding evident. The jeep jolted along as more and more bumps presented themselves.

During the next few days those about Jeron were busy preparing for some eventuality, the purpose of which was kept from him. He had the feeling that although he was being treated courteously by all whom he met, he was not accepted as entirely trustworthy and consequently this did not improve his general attitude towards the court of Serainis. The only encouragement he received was the amiable conversations with Tiros and the quiet company of Yola who gently refused to let a closer relationship form under the present conditions. The most he could achieve was to occasionally hold her hand as they walked around the environs of the keep, but with a little smile she would even withdraw this slight link if other people appeared on the scene. It irritated him that he had to observe such formal behaviour for the benefit of others whilst his own frustration increased. He longed to tell Yola of his feelings and take her away from this place, but he was forced to respect her wishes.

Other thoughts preyed on his mind also. The mystery of his past and the lost memory must be somehow tied up with the strong interest he had in Serainis. The same type of obsessive feeling had led him to investigate the Tower of Pandilex. Something had made him suddenly move his hand to the design on the central pillar, to release the death of Raitis. That was no magic of his, he felt sure. It was as if his mind had been abruptly manipulated by some external force. He seemed to be under a curse which stopped him acting entirely as himself. Was it possible that this curse could be removed by some person skilled in such matters of the mind? Perhaps Serainis herself might help him. He was much in awe of her but maybe if he confided his problem to her, she might in turn respect his trust and make his life here more bearable. Her courtiers would then accept him and possibly Yola would allow him to pursue his attentions more openly.

Jeron spoke to her of his decision to ask Serainis for help. She was obviously pleased that he had decided to put his trust in her superior and told him that there was nobody so learned in the arts of power, unless one counted Ina, the old witch of the Dead Forest. That old woman might still be alive although none had seen her for some years now. Ina had been alive when Pandilex was in his youth, and had acted as his tutor before the sorcerer's own powers had gained their reputation.

So Jeron asked to see Serainis for a private audience and this was granted. When he arrived at her apartments in the castle he was ushered into a small but richly decorated chamber. The diminutive girl servant withdrew after instructing him to wait there. In a little while he became aware of an overwhelming presence although he could not see the person and he guessed that she was looking at him from some secret spyhole before making herself known. This was probably correct, for when he turned around Serainis was standing there, pushing back the long, jet-black hair which swept over her white shoulders. A deep blue gown sheathed her body and Jeron admired the sheer elegance of the siren before him. She spoke in that cold voice peculiar to her.

'Welcome to these my humble quarters. I have been looking forward to speaking alone with you and it seems from what Yola has told me that perhaps I may now be of some service to you. Indeed as one who has twice saved the life of my trusted follower you hold us all in your debt. I shall endeavour to do whatever lies within my power to repay your timely acts. Tell me then exactly how I may help you.'

She smiled at him and his pulse leapt. Without doubt the feelings that she induced in him were abnormal in their intensity. He tried desperately to maintain a calm composure, but the longer he stayed in her presence, the more he was physically attracted to her.

'Lady Serainis, I am much honoured that you should consider helping me. My problems, as you may know, stem from the inability to recall anything that happened prior to my initial appearance before Yola. Although since then I have apparently commanded powers of high potency and thereby ended the life of Raitis, yet I fail to understand how I accomplished such action. It would seem that there are times when my actions are ordered by a mind other than my own. Without doubt if there is a key to this problem of mine, you will surely find it, for I am much in awe of your considerable reputation.'

She smiled thinly, apparently pleased with his words, and

approaching nearer to him, put her cool hands upon his forehead.

'Worry not, Jeron. I shall delve deeper into your mind than any have done before. This will cause you some discomfort if you do not relax completely. Therefore make your mind receptive in that when you feel the touch of my seeking mind do not repel as is the instinctive way, but instead attempt to remain passive. In this way the greatest advance may be made and the barrier set in your mind may be overcome. Do you understand?'

Jeron assented and for a moment nothing happened. The lovely face drew close to his and her subtle perfume stole over him as the hypnotic eyes held his attention. Then inside his mind a terrible, sickening pressure developed. His ears rang as the tension increased. Before him the green eyes of Serainis grew in size and ever-widening pools enveloped him. Wave after wave of terrible agony bore into his mind until he cried out with pain. Suddenly his whole being shook as he forcefully rejected the intruder from his body. There was extreme blackness and then he passed out. Serainis tottered back a few steps and then recovered her balance. She eyed the unconscious man at her feet and gently pushed his head to one side with her dainty shoe.

'So that is where you get your defences from, my visitor from afar. It seems that there is one considerably stronger than you, who has set these spells to counteract any mind examination. Even so the barriers only hold as long as Jeron himself can reject me. Well, there is another way, which once achieved will enable me to draw the truth out with minimum of effort. The elixir of Kyrrod has a terribly persuasive way.' She smiled and went out of the room to return a moment later with a small phial of red liquid. A few drops of this were added to some wine, and Serainis carefully poured this mixture down Jeron's throat.

He awoke to find her bending over him. She smiled sweetly.

'My poor friend, I fear that the psychic blocks in your mind are more firmly set than I had anticipated. Still, they give signs of weakness and will surely collapse if you can add your will to mine. For this purpose it is necessary that you drop all reservations and in spite of our short acquaintance, place all your trust in me. What I am about to attempt will only work if your will and mine are one. Therefore if you are still keen to break through you must do exactly as I say. Fill your mind completely with thoughts of me. Accept me not just as your friend, but completely as part of yourself. Allow me to enter and fill your mind and body with the essence of my being. Do not resist or be afraid, but rather welcome this temporary possession, secure in the absolute trust you place in me. As an unborn child relies totally on the safety and security of its mother's womb, so shall you yield yourself completely to me. In this way our strengths and wills shall be more than doubled, and so unified we shall break open the walls set across your memory. Will you do this, Jeron, for remember that having done so there shall be no secrets of yours hidden from my seeking mind?'

Something in Jeron's mind began to scream at him with a message of urgency, but the wine that Serainis had given to him slowed his reactions surprisingly, so that he felt withdrawn and passive. Vaguely he wondered at the noise inside him, but with every moment it elicited less and less response. Serainis's sharp eyes held his attention, for they again began to fill his vision. He heard a voice speaking from his lips assenting to her suggestion and making promises in reply to her cross-examination. Then he stopped speaking and knew that he was committed to her experiment.

Her glittering eyes held his attention. The last small effort of resistance deserted him and he found himself submitting completely to her. Serainis drew him towards her and placed her red lips upon his forehead, her hands holding his. She pursed her lips and a great weakness came over Jeron, as, like some awful parasite, she sucked all the will from him. His legs tottered and she helped him to lie down upon a couch. Gradually he lost all awareness of his surroundings, and life itself hardly flickered within his body. Then the mind of Serainis, exuberant in her mighty power, entered into him and possessed him utterly. A feeling of bubbling, writhing force swept through his being like a whirlwind passing through a forest of leaves. Terrible, evil thoughts crossed his mind. The remnant of himself shuddered and recoiled from the deadly invasion. A mind looked out through his eyes that was a hybrid of himself and the possessor.

The whole thing was wrong, completely sickening. He should never have agreed to let himself be captured so easily. Even as he thought this, the other part of his mind screamed with laughter. Something snapped within his agonised mind. He remembered now the purpose of his interest in Serainis. He had been sent by one infinitely more powerful than he to seek her out and ascertain her personality, to kill her if needs be, for total evil was not allowable at any cost. Who was it that had sent him? Why, yes, he could remember now. He who had sent him had been named Pandilex, greatest of all the seers. His mind was cast in an agony of pain as a multitude of questions were thrust at him. Suddenly the interrogation ceased and Serainis vacated his mind. His strength only partly returned to him however, although he succeeded after some dizziness in sitting up on the couch.

She stood before him and only a glance was needed to see that she knew far more about him and his past than he could ever know himself. An amused smile lit her beautiful face and he wondered what would happen to him now. No doubt the easiest refutation of Pandilex's intentions was simply to kill him. Why then did she hesitate?

'Well, friend Jeron, it seems that I did well to probe your mysteries. We have apparently little basis for mutual trust in our relationship. You have revealed to me all that I wish to know. Because of my devious father, you are a personal threat to me as long as you remain alive, for even I cannot revoke the course he set you on. It is a great pity, for you display qualities which I find most interesting, but regretfully I must stop you in a very final way from completing the task of your master. You must see that I cannot be satisfied with a mere assurance from you that no threat is implied, for I have read your thoughts and know the mission that my father sent you upon. Yes, Jeron, you may well look dejected, for I have no alternative but to kill you for my own peace of mind.

'Unfortunately your death would raise questions by others in my court, unless you left more naturally. Therefore I shall give leave for your beloved Yola to go on a journey with you, apparently on behalf of our cause. At a certain point in the journey I shall release to you the residue of will power that is yours, and which at present I hold within my spirit. This you shall use to effect the deaths of Yola and yourself. Since death in itself is little punishment for the threat which you present to me, you will suffer all the more because of the fore-knowledge of your inevitable end. To Yola you will be unable to communicate any warning, for I have set a barrier which binds your lips in this respect only. Within three days from now I and the court will be amazed to hear the sad news of your deaths, and we shall mourn the loss of such good friends to the cause. Go now and prepare for your last journey. I shall now summon your companion and given her an explanation for this travel.'

She went over to the nearest wall and pulled on a bellrope. Jeron found his legs taking him towards an exit. It was obvious that she had his body under control as easily as manipulating a puppet. There seemed little point in struggling against the iron determination of his limbs and if he had to fight for self-control it would be better to do so when his mind had rested awhile from the ordeals with Serainis.

He was packed and ready with two horses in the castle courtyard when Yola joined him. She greeted him with a ready smile and gave him an explanation of their mission dictated to her by Serainis. He chatted back easily enough, but after a few unsuccessful attempts to warn her about Serainis, at which times his speech came out in words completely different from those he had intended, he desisted, and instead gave profound thought to his problems. It was clear that sooner or later he would involuntarily do something which would put them both in mortal peril, if Serainis had her way. How could he avoid this?

Yola looked at her riding companion out of the corners of her eyes. He was certainly very handsome and she knew that his feelings for her were strong and noble as well. Still, it did not do to encourage him too quickly, for once he realised exactly how she felt about him, it would be difficult, if not impossible, to maintain the strict working relationship that was necessary in order to carry out the mission with clear heads, alert for signs of danger on the way. The quality of uncertainty meant that he could not take her feelings for granted, and so respect was maintained. Also there were too many mysteries about Jeron for Yola to readily accept him without question. If only she could help to solve his problems for him, then there should be few obstacles in the way of their relationship.

It had been somewhat disappointing when Serainis had told her that more time was needed before she could read into his past. Yola ducked as they rode past a low tree bough. Serainis had asked for a message to be delivered to Ludin, who commanded a small force of soldiers at the extreme end of the Three Forests. She wrinkled her nose in disgust at the thought of the ride. The first two forests were bad enough for riding through, because of their density of growth, but the last one was the Dead Forest where nothing lived, except perhaps the Old Crone. Provided they kept to the one path through the Dead Forest, little harm should come to them, but rumour had it that trespassers soon discovered that the Forest was not so dead as it looked.

CHAPTER SEVEN

The following day they cleared the Second Forest as it was known, and after a brief interval riding through moorland, they entered into the Dead Forest. Dry twigs cracked like whips as the horses pushed forward. Strange, tall hulks of empty tree shells met them on all sides. Once, a very long time ago, there had been masses of thick greenery striving upwards to greet the light. Now all was grey and lifeless. A thick dust covered the petrified trees and the ground was overspread with the same strange ash. An eerie silence hung over the whole area, and the travellers could see no signs of any wild life present.

At one point they came across a vast number of giant trees of such immense proportions that the tops were lost out of sight in some low cloud. The bases of the wide trunks split up into numerous thick roots, which dipped and rose out of the ground every few yards, making progress difficult. Once they saw evidence of life in some former age as they passed the ruins of a round stone tower. Jeron was keen to investigate this further, but Yola had an intuitive feeling that danger lurked there and she dissuaded him. They made haste to leave the area and soon had left it behind them.

Later that day the path which they had been following grew thinner and then stopped abruptly at a circular area surrounded by trees. From various angles other paths led off into the woods again.

'Now what do we do?' asked Jeron, somewhat bad-temperedly, for his inability to warn the girl of the danger that he represented had never left his mind during the journey.

She looked at him down-heartedly. As far as she knew there only existed one traveller's road through the Dead Forest. It had not occurred to her that there might be cross-roads or complex junctions such as this one. Where to go from here?

'We must have deviated from the original path. I thought only one route through the woods was available, but now it seems as if a whole network of such roads has been created.' She frowned, there was something not quite right about some of the roads as she regarded them, for they appeared to move almost imperceptibly like huge and deadly serpents waiting for the unwary to step too close. Jeron felt a weak but persistent voice in his mind, as if shouting from a great distance. As he tried desperately to catch the urgent message, he found to his horror that his lips had been speaking all the while to Yola, and that even now he was leading her confidently towards one of the alternative roads. An awakening sense of imminent disaster burst upon his understanding, as he strove to regain control of his movements. They walked up to the road he had indicated to Yola, but although he fought with every effort in his will, his outward appearance gave no sign of the inner conflict between mind and body. A pace away and he screamed inside himself as all his senses rebelled against each other. This is it, he thought in despair, Serainis has won and now we go to our death in some awful way. Oh, forgive me, my dearest Yola, you will never know how I led you unwittingly to your fate.

'No, I think this is the wrong way, Jeron. Let's try the road over there. I have a strange feeling about this one. Come on.' She turned around and suddenly the pressure on his mind was relaxed once more. Perhaps her sudden change of mind had taken Serainis by surprise and upset the influence the sorceress exerted upon her victim. If so, then perhaps there was some hope after all, for there were many unpredictable things about this Dead Forest.

'Hurry,' urged Yola, 'we must get away from the Forest before nightfall. The horses need water and I doubt whether any can be found hereabouts.' She spurred her horse and they went forward again. As they did so they saw that the path ahead bore various symbols written on it in a manner that confused the eyes.

'I don't know what the purpose of these signs is, but so long as this way leads out of the Forest I don't mind,' said Yola. Jeron remained silent but nodded in reply. The influence of Serainis was still with him, of that he was sure. Somehow he had to warn Yola about what had happened between Serainis and himself, but every time he contrived to devise a message his thoughts were read instantly and his intentions thwarted by some twist of his tongue, or temporary paralysis of his limbs. At this very instant Serainis was listening to his meditations.

A little later they came across a second cross-roads, and Yola suggested that they continue travelling straight ahead. They applied this principle also when a third cross-roads presented itself and in this way kept the shadows behind them each time a choice of routes was offered. As they stepped on the chosen paths the ground ahead glowed with symbols carved in the same manner as those they had seen earlier. At last the path began to spiral inwards in great sweeps, until they suddenly came across a clearing in the middle of which stood a great stone house.

This curious building was made up from many interlocking triangular pieces of rock, and was all the more interesting because the walls leaned inwards like a pyramid, although at a lesser angle, so that the roof was much smaller in area than the ground floor. Jeron went to go forward to investigate this strange house, but Yola pulled him back.

'Be careful,' she whispered, 'the inhabitants may not be of a friendly disposition. Who would choose to live here in such dismal surroundings unless they were abnormal in some frightful way? It would be better to return the way we came rather than run the risk of alerting anyone of our presence here in these woods.'

He drew back his arm impatiently. 'How far do you think we could go without food and water for the horses and ourselves? This wood is a maze of paths and I doubt whether retracing our steps is quite so simple as you think. We don't even know the correct direction to make for. There is really not much alternative for us but to ask for help here. Still, don't look so glum, Yola, for the people inside may well be friendly.'

'I doubt it, but if you have made up your mind to go in, then will I come too, for I do not fancy spending time alone in this sinister Dead Forest.'

They tied their horses to a tree stump, and made their way over to the quaint stone house. No one replied to their knocking on the door, or their shouts, so they went inside. A simple room that served both as a kitchen and living-room greeted them. A single line of steps followed the circular interior of the walls and led upstairs. As Jeron stood there looking about him, he suddenly felt to his horror a crushing pressure inside his head. For a moment he tried to withstand the driving force within him, but the agony increased relentlessly and the last efforts of resistance were overcome.

He grabbed Yola's hand and dragged her up the steps despite her protestations. Almost as if his own mind had withdrawn as a mere onlooker, he found that his actions were completely beyond his control. He was dominated utterly by Serainis's influence.

'Stop it, Jeron. You are hurting my wrist. Whatever is the matter with you?' shouted Yola as she struggled to wrestle free from his iron grip. 'Please let me go. I don't know what you are trying to do. Oh, Jeron, aren't you my friend any more?' For the first time in his company she was afraid of him. He had a strange, far-away look on his face as if he no longer heard her entreaties. He said nothing, but clamping his arms about her thin waist, lifted her from the steps and advanced up into the room above. This contained little in the way of furniture. A pile of old books stood on a table, and some fell to the floor as Yola struggled violently to free herself, but she was held fast by the strong arms. Jeron kicked aside a rocking chair and bore her over to the long vertical window which was set into the stone wall. She shrieked as she suddenly realised his intentions. The window was thrown open and with a mighty effort he stepped up on to the thin ledge which overlooked the sloping stone walls of the curiously shaped house. The walls were constructed of many triangular pieces of rock, and where they interlocked, a large number of the stones had become displaced with age, so that the steeply inclining walls contained hundreds of sharp-edged pieces jutting out at all angles. The moment after they fell down the sides of the house, the sharp stone knives would cut them into ribbons before they crashed into the rock surround at the base of the house.

'Jeron, for pity's sake, we shall both be killed if you do not get back. Oh, do you not love me any more? What is it that has happened to you; how can you have changed so quickly and so dreadfully?'

Jeron bent her back further and further over the edge. Slowly they began to topple forwards. Yola screamed, her reason beginning to desert her, whilst inside the room the air stirred and the form of an old woman became visible on the rocking chair. She was frail and withered, old beyond conjecture, but her eyes were very, very sharp and they saw the horror within the blankness of Jeron's face as his body moved like a robot.

The old witch spoke in a strange tongue and the couple froze in their action. She got up slowly and walked over to where they stood on the edge of the window ledge and regarded them in stony silence, her face impassive as her eyes darted from one to the other. A cold, withered hand was put on Jeron's forehead and then Yola's mind was explored. Ina returned to her chair and released them from their bondage.

'Welcome to this my home,' she said ironically, 'but stand back from the window lest the view entice you over the edge of sanity.' They both began to speak at once, but she cut them short with a wave of her hand. 'You forget that I have read your minds and therefore no explanations are necessary to me. However it seems, young man, that an explanation is owed to your lady friend, for it is not every day that a young woman is paid compliments in the compelling fashion that you provide. Tell her then all that you know of Serainis, for it is the least that you owe her.' The old witch muttered some words in a low voice and he found that the influence upon him set by Serainis had gone completely. He looked at Yola, who had moved to the other side of the room away from him, and now regarded him with a fearful countenance. He went over, and taking her hand more gently this time, begged her forgiveness, explaining how Serainis had spell-bound him to prevent any warning of their intended death.

Yola could hardly believe her ears as the truth about the intentions of her superior were made clear. For many years the young girl had worked without question on behalf of Serainis. Did this mean that all the tasks which she had done for her leader were evil? She could not believe so, and yet the evidence before her seemed to conflict with any alternative. Could Jeron, whom she knew very little about, be really trusted just because she had taken a liking to this tall stranger who had saved her life? Perhaps he never had lost his memory at all, and perhaps he was some unknown enemy of Serainis, determined to use Yola in some way now that his murder attempt had failed.

'Nor is that all the story,' said the old woman, 'for Serainis had such a strong interest in you that she would have killed you both, even though one of you has served her well and faithfully in the past. We shall delve back much further in this mystery, for I can see that many questions have still to be answered. Indeed I am not sure that your lady has yet forgiven you, young man, so you both would do well to listen to me. Come with me and see what I can find for you that will restore your shaken faith in each other.'

She took out a key and unlocked a small wooden door set into one of the walls. They stooped below the low entrance and found themselves inside a room packed with objects, the purpose of which they were at a complete loss to explain. It seemed that there was no limit to the utter complexity of magic, Yola thought, as she eyed the shelves of potions and powders, bottles of peculiar liquids and ointments, and strange machines. From a dark corner the old woman brought a large, circular, shallow bowl which she placed on a small table in the centre of the room. Jeron was asked to hand down a glass bottle from one of the shelves, and from this was poured a dark green liquid. The surface of this shimmered and twisted about as if it were alive, although after a while it settled down to a smooth, mirror-like surface. As the two of them watched, the witch spoke to the liquid and asked Jeron to touch the surface lightly. He did so and a strange world looked out at them from the interior of the bowl, a room filled with books, so many that Yola thought they must be all those ever written. Jeron saw a tiny replica of himself, speaking in a foreign tongue to another man. The aged witch spoke softly to the bowl and the picture faded gradually to be replaced by that of a book, tattered and damaged, which Jeron was reading excitedly. As they strained their eyes trying to catch the details on the pages, Yola gave a surprised exclamation, for there in one of the pictures was a painting of herself.

To Jeron it seemed as if the images he saw of himself were

not real, but dream-like. He hadn't recognised anything. He felt disappointed although his curiosity in the visions remained. Presumably if his memory was affected adversely then he would have to accept without question the message of the pictures in the bowl. A series of scenes grew and faded in turn as they watched the green liquid in total silence. Eventually the witch carefully poured the liquid back into its container, and gave it to Jeron who placed it up on the shelf again. Ina looked at their anxious faces and smiled a little. Then she told them the whole of the story, as the bowl had told her in its own peculiar way.

Jeron was a man from another world in another time, summoned by dead Pandilex to assess the innocence or guilt of Serainis, and if necessary to act as the instrument of justice. Yola began to realise how she had misjudged Jeron, and that his recent actions against herself may well have been involuntary if Serainis had regarded him as an enemy to be quickly disposed of.

'Does Serainis realise all this too?' asked the girl, thinking of the strange powers of her leader.

'Some of the story possibly, but not all,' was the reply.

'Even so she must have found out enough to know that Jeron's death would be an advantage and that as his friend I could also represent a possible danger.'

'True,' acknowledged the old woman, 'but had she realised the full story then the last thing she would have tried to do would be to assassinate your friend here.'

'Why? I don't see how I could be of any value to her.' Jeron shrugged his shoulders. The witch gave him a caustic look in return.

'Think harder, young man, or do not think at all. Serainis, in order to win a decisive battle against her rivals Tokin and Zaduk the Deviant, needs larger armies of soldiers with weapons against whose might her enemies are powerless.

Surely you can imagine her thoughts if she knew that there existed a means whereby men from another time-world could enter into this one to boost her armies, whether willingly or otherwise. Once she realises that where you came from was not just a far off part of this planet, but a completely different civilisation with unusual knowledge and powers, then she will do all in her power to regain you as a prisoner and force the truth from you. Now that you consciously know your origins the mental blocks on your memory will have gone, and she will read your part in all this as easily as any adept in the powers could do. From that moment on it will be but a matter of time before the way to your own world is found and her evil influence asserts itself there.' Ina sighed. This man had unwittingly acted as a pawn in the game played between Serainis and dead Pandilex, and would bring bad luck to this world and his own unless he was very careful.

'What can we do then,' begged Yola, looking from one to the other, 'for sooner or later Serainis and her forces will surely find us?' Even now it seemed strange to her that she should be hunted by those who a little while ago were her friends.

Ina thought for a while and then spoke again. 'Whilst Jeron and you are susceptible to capture, not only are you both in danger of your lives once the truth is out, but also Jeron's world and its people are threatened. Somehow we must find a way back before Serainis can find you, and therefore we must send both of you from this globe, never to return. In that way your problems may be solved. Indeed should you discover how to get back, do not tell me, for though my powers are still alive, yet I grow weaker with age and time, and I would not welcome a visit from Serainis these days. Thus you must leave me before her spies find you here with me. It seems to me that you need some help if you are to evade Serainis and find the way back to Jeron's world. My knowledge does not stretch to matters such as the latter, but perhaps I can give you some protection and some advice.

'In the days when this forest was alive and green, there were beings so powerful in the arts of sorcery that Serainis and myself would have been considered mere novices. Unfortunately these people were subject to the same defects of human nature as ourselves, and lived in continual conflict with each other. One terrible day there was a gathering of power so intense that lesser mortals fled, or, like myself, hid themselves from the sight of that display of strength. When all was finished, we crept out from our hiding places, like insects after a storm, and were amazed to see that all the world about us was white. There was no colour in the trees or on the ground, only dead, bleached wood of a forest grave-yard. After a few days those left behind with me decided to disperse, and so I stayed alone in the lifeless forest. Still, I was not without resources and after a little while contrived to build a home to live in, for my former house had suffered like the others in my area. Also it suited me to stay in this dead place in order to continue my studies quietly, and to meditate without interruption.

'Often subsequently I wondered what had happened to the superior beings who had warred too often against each other, but only once did I find a reminder of their former presence. Of their homes no trace existed except that the white dust was thicker there, but one day as I drew water from the stream that still remained uncontaminated despite the surroundings, my eyes caught a sparkle of red in the gravel. It was a ring made from a curious red metal that was worn only by the vanished race. When my fingers touched it, a thrill ran through me as if the ring possessed some power unknown to me.

'Now this ring you shall have, for it seems to me that only those not of this world are fit to wear the token of this former race. I do not understand its function, save that energy in great amounts is absorbed and stored within it, and may be released from time to time, but when exactly this may be I cannot tell, for it does not obey my commands. Still when you find that power is being released, then use it to accomplish that which you have to do and thereby save your own strength and will.

'I promised you advice as well. This is it. I do not know how you may effect entry to your world, Jeron, although Pandilex knew of such things. However answers of a kind may be given to all questions, if one puts them to the voice within the Bottomless Well of Amphor.' She paused and drank from a wine flask.

'But where is that? Where can we find this place?' asked Jeron eagerly. The witch smiled at his directness. She went over to a wooden box in the corner of the room and after sorting through the varied contents, returned with a long roll of animal skin. This she placed on the floor in front of them and unrolled it to reveal a crude and ancient map. The old woman laughed at their eager faces and jabbed the map with a bony forefinger.

'Many have sought Amphor's Well but only a handful have succeeded. Some say that it is hidden under the Lake of Crystals at Bakuth here, whilst others deny this and testify to its presence at Thorg. Some people even say that it is here at the Desert of Sirl, though many deny its existence at all and declare it but a folk tale.' She looked up at them and paused for a moment. 'They are all wrong. Accept advice from one who has been there and come back. As far as I know it is still there deep within the Tomb of the Twins, inside the Hill of Death. At Karpon on the map here, there is an artificial mound greatly feared by all who live near. Anyone who enters the Tomb of the Twins must first protect himself from the evil within by cutting himself with a knife and offering up a cup of blood to that dread thing called the Guardian. Once this is done and the blood sacrifice is accepted, the Guardian sleeps for a short while, and in that time one must proceed to the Well and ask one question only for each of you. Do not delay, for if you are still within the Tomb when that evil creature awakes, then your flesh will perish in a way beyond all imagining. Take this ring from my hand and also this map, and remember it is better to trust no one than to accept an enemy within your company by some foolish act of friendship. Go now before Serainis and her spies come for you.'

They thanked her for the gifts and advice, and set off according to the map. Jeron placed the ring on his second finger and was disappointed not to feel anything from the band of red metal. There were many tiny characters engraved into the sides but none were familiar to Yola. With the help of the map they soon found their way out of the Dead Forest and into the living countryside again.

Many miles away Serainis sat trance-like in her castle, as in her queer green eyes a picture was reflected of the two travellers as they journeyed onwards. The scene faded as she arose from her couch and summoned Tiros to meet her immediately.

CHAPTER EIGHT

Many days passed and now a new kind of relationship developed between the two friends, for the mystery about Jeron which had caused a certain amount of reserve between them, had been solved. Although the dangers that surrounded them were very real, their common purpose drew them closer together, and their friendship blossomed into a much deeper feeling for each other. During the journey to Karpon, which by itself would have been long and tedious, they chatted eagerly with each other at length about all sorts of topics, finding that they had much in common even though their lives had obviously been so different. Many times Jeron would endeavour to bring the subject around to his love for Yola, but she being wiser in such matters, would skilfully turn the conversation back to more mundane topics, lest their strong emotions became carried away in youthful passion.

As they came at last towards the end of their journey, the land of Karpon came in sight, and thus proved the validity of their map. This was a hot, dry place where the ground was cracked from the exposure to the suns, and the sparse vegetation was brown and withered. Here the road was littered with many small rocks whereon sat strange-looking lizards and other creatures sunning themselves. These moved away quickly as the riders drew near and their darting movements caused the horses to shy uneasily. From the skin map they saw that the Tomb of the Twins lay a further half mile ahead of them beyond a broken line of hills. They were setting off again after their short rest when they heard a shout behind them as in the distance a horse and rider came towards them. Jeron frowned and drew out his short sword as a precaution, but Yola whose eyes were sharper than his, placed her hand on his arm.

'Put down your sword, my aggressive friend. It's Tiros!'

Tiros it was indeed, covered with dust and plainly exhausted. He greeted them wearily. As soon as he had recovered his breath, he told them that he and Evran had left Serainis's court after being warned by friends that soldiers were coming to arrest them because of their association with Jeron and Yola. Evran had sustained several deep wounds in getting away from a sudden confrontation of armed horsemen, and he was now resting in the shade of some trees further back down the road.

They turned their horses back and travelled along the dusty trail. Whilst Yola and Tiros were engaged in conversation Jeron was left to his thoughts. Why was Ginah not mentioned as fleeing from the court? How had Tiros managed to get clear away whilst Evran had apparently suffered badly? His suspicions increased as he saw that Tiros's horse was still fairly fresh despite the road dust that covered it and the rider. If the horse had ridden at the pace indicated by Tiros for that distance, then it should have been in very poor shape. This indicated that a relay of horses had been used, yet there should have been no time to organise such fresh transport. Jeron tightened his grip on the sword as they came nearer to the group of trees indicated by Tiros as Evran's resting place. He caught the others up and nudged Yola's arm, indicating his suspicions to her by a worried look. She probed his mind and caught his meaning. Her horse slowed a little so that Tiros went on ahead of them.

'Be prepared to turn back quickly. I think this may well be some kind of a trap. Whatever happens ride back along the trail as fast as you can. I shall try to hold them off for a while.'

She nodded and then smiled at Tiros who had stopped and was waiting for them to catch up with him. There was an ominous silence from the thick growth of bushes and trees on either side of him.

Yola stared hard at Tiros, whose face was set like a mask. Oh no, she thought to herself, not you, not my old friend of a thousand battles. Where is that honest smile now? She tried to enter his mind but there was no space there, someone had already got there before her. Someone she knew very well. Her heart bled with bitterness. Now the only true friend she had was Jeron.

'Evran, old comrade, we are here!' shouted Tiros to the trees, and from the thick cover rose a small company of armed soldiers.

'Ride!' shouted Jeron, as he hacked at the nearest of the oncoming soldiers. Yola's horse plunged back and jumped clear over the only attacker between her and the open road. Jeron's sword turned crimson as he plunged it into the man's neck. With an effort he pulled the bloody weapon free from the corpse and rode down another man. Tiros, his eyes wide and staring madly, lunged at him but missed his balance and his frightened horse took off in another direction. Jeron's horse followed Yola's as behind them the disorganised company regathered for pursuit.

'The Tomb,' yelled Jeron to the girl ahead of him, 'we must get there before they can catch up with us.'

'It's over there between the gap in the hills,' she gasped, her throat dry with the clouds of dust. 'The map said so.'

Their tired horses struggled to keep their pace as the road began to incline upwards. Over and through the yawning gap between the high surrounding hills they went, and then suddenly in front of them stood the Hill of Death. A large mound of black soil rose before them and at the base stood a stone archway, on either side of which were engraved two figures of mythical beasts with repulsive reptilian heads. There was no door, just a dark gap between the archway. A faint cold breeze stirred on the hillside and caused Yola to shiver. Her initial courage began to ebb as she examined the blackness of the entrance to the tomb. There was no sign of the Guardian mentioned by Ina, but then they had not yet stepped inside. Behind them the sounds of their pursuers grew.

'Come,' said Jeron determinedly, taking her firmly by the hand, 'now is not the time to hesitate. Let's get this over with. The danger within may or may not be real, but the danger behind us is certainly apparent.' She smiled at him, glad that he was taking the role of leader, and giving her no time to let her fears grow out of proportion. He took out the small wine cups that the old witch had given them and scratched their arms with the point of his sword. The blood was collected in the cups, and they quickly bound each other's wounds with strips of cloth from the hem of her dress. Feeling very anxious about the approaching soldiers, Jeron placed the cups at the entrance to the tomb, and using the witch's instructions, cut down a long branch from one of the trees near by. This he used to push the cups within the tomb out of sight completely. He withdrew the branch, as from inside the darkness there was a metallic clang as one of the cups fell to the floor, followed a few seconds later by the other. White-faced, they stared at each other, and then as the horsemen rode up to the mouth of the tomb, Yola was pulled by Jeron into the interior.

Tiros sprang from his frothing mount and ran to the dark entrance, but stopped there, sensing that evil lay within. Softly spoken commands whispered in his brain, as the one he feared looked through his eyes at the scene. His body responded, as sword in hand, he advanced into the dense black interior after the other two. Outside the band of soldiers waited silently with grim faces. They knew what it was to be possessed. Now Tiros was experiencing the dread split between the natural and the invading will. No one could withstand that terrifying, malignant take-over. Once it had happened something in the original personality died, and long after the process was over, there was a vacuum where part of the spirit had been, as if the contact with the entering evil had burnt and scarred the soul irreparably. All those who were of that élite group of men called the Guard of Serainis wore the same grey look within their eyes.

Tiros began to panic at the thought of the unknown with which he would be in company. Something told him that here was horror far greater than anything he had ever experienced before, but though he strained his eyes he could see nothing stirring in the dim light around him. His scalp began to crawl with terror as he imagined the close proximity of the unmentionable. He struggled to retreat, but Serainis squeezed his brain harder in the icy talons of her will, and forced him to go on.

Somewhere on the far side of the Universe, Taylor stared unbelievingly at the smoke issuing forth from under the bonnet. His muscles ached as he eased himself out of the seat and carefully opened up the hot metal casing. Smoke bellowed forth and to his dismay he saw that the engine was a complete write-off. A light flickered for an instant in the interior, and he hastily jumped back as a sheet of flame flared up. With sinking heart, he sat on the dune opposite, and watched the funeral pyre of his chariot. When it was all over, he went back and poked amongst the charred remains with his shoes, but there was nothing of any practical use left for him. Despite the warmth he shivered. The sky was getting brighter again. Soon the terrifying heat of the sun would bear down upon him and begin the slow process of desiccating his tissues and body fluids unless he found shelter. There was no scenic clue available to decide which way offered the best hope. The way he had come offered none.

He got up and started walking. The grains of sand crumbled beneath his feet, and he lurched off-balance every now and then. Surely it couldn't be far off. That damned mast must be visible over the next dune dammit. How much slower this punitive walking was compared with the progress of the jeep. He would have been almost half a mile away by now, whereas he was still not over the first golden ridge yet. The sun rose in its majestic glory over the dunes behind him and warmed the skin on his neck. At least he was lucky in that respect, for he was not marching against the sun. How long one could survive such conditions he didn't know, but he began to remember the dinner-time jokes in the mess about people who went for a stroll in the desert. They didn't seem quite so funny in the present context.

Now he was scrambling up and on to the top of the shifting dust. Another hill of sand greeted him, exactly the twin of the one he was standing on. Just beyond it he could see the summit of another. Taylor closed his aching eyes for a moment to shut out the glare of the light and then continued down the slope. It would have been so nice to have sat there and rested awhile, but he knew that he was now racing against time. The longer he remained exposed to the powerful sun the more certain it was that sunstroke or thirst would kill him. He had no choice but to keep moving. The only sound he heard was his own laboured breathing.

As their eyes became more accustomed to the darkness of the tomb they saw that ahead of them lay a long passage inclining downwards, carved out of solid rock. Their footsteps echoed hollowly as they ventured further downwards. The ground was slippery due to a thin but constant stream of water flowing under their feet. From time to time they saw skeletons on the ground, many twisted and warped as if the people they had once been had met their death crouching in abject terror. Several times Yola thought she would faint, but her companion's strong arms held her closely to his side, and she drew comfort from his courage.

As they walked along a sound met their ears. This regularly grew in intensity and then diminished, and they soon realised that they were walking towards it. A kind of wheezing groan issued forth from a chamber ahead of them on their right. Yola gasped in fear and clutched Jeron tightly. The shadow of the Guardian lay across the ground in front of them. The size of the creature must have been enormous, but the actual shape was difficult to make out from the shadow. They edged forward on the opposite side. As Yola looked across and saw that which slept there, she fainted with horror, and Jeron caught her slight body as she collapsed. He lifted her up and was careful not to look at the nightmare of evil which lay only feet away from them. Only one part did he see out of the corner of his eye and he realised with a shock that what he had taken at first glance to be the thick fingers of a giant hand, were in fact monstrous types of suckers, from which some of their blood offering still oozed. It must have moved extremely silently to have drunk from the blood cups and moved back to its sleeping place without a sound. Just how long it would stay asleep he did not know. Presumably the small meal they had offered would not satisfy it for very long. He staggered past the dread giant and a little further on managed to revive Yola.

'It's all right, my dear,' he said earnestly to her, 'we are past that dreadful thing. Can you manage to walk now? We must hurry now before it wakes again, for our time is limited. The Well must be ahead somewhere.'

She was still trembling from the shock. She pushed her long red hair back from her face and tried to compose herself. 'Oh, Jeron, what terrible mind could create such a horror to guard this Tomb? Surely nothing human could devise such terror. Take me quickly from here lest I faint again at the thought of it. If it should awake and all seems lost, then kill me with your sword, for I would sooner die at your own dear hands than by that awful, unclean death.'

On they went and the passage grew higher and wider. Soon the rough walls became smoother as the artistic creations of a bygone age became apparent. Painted on the walls were scenes of a world long ago, where strange beasts and trees of enormous height were evident. Nowhere on any of these great wall-panels were pictures of man to be seen, although signs of an intelligence equal or superior to man were displayed in the great stone buildings and monuments depicted in the murals. Some of the latter claimed Jeron's interest. Huge flat stones rested upon pairs of vertical support rocks. Long ago he had seen something like this but the memory of it was hazy. There the overall arrangement of the triads had been circular, rather than triangular as was the case here.

They hurried along and found that the passage turned to the left, and then right again, and they found themselves in an immense underground cavern so vast that they could not see the roof in the dim light. In the middle of this cavern stood two thick grey columns which terminated some twenty feet above the ground level. Jeron was looking to see where the exit was that might lead to the Well when Yola took his hand excitedly and pointed to the base of the columns.

'Look,' she exclaimed, 'don't you see? These are the Twins. Is that not a foot where you are looking, and that over there another one?'

He stared at the base of the column and saw the great thick clawlike toes of the dead being who towered above him. Due to its great age, the skin had mummified into a hard shell-like material and some of the features had become blunted as parts of the exterior had collapsed with the passing of time. Its twin fellow was in a similar state although at some stage in its history the head had received some terrible wounds from a sharp instrument. The faces were strangely reptilian, though the features displayed signs of intelligence.

Yola dragged Jeron away from his study of these ancient

relics of a bygone past and led him towards a small chamber set into the side of the great Tomb of the Twins. Here a small series of steps led down to the remains of a stone altar. Set in front of this was a raised circular layer of green crystalline rock, and looking over this Jeron realised that at last they had found the bottomless Well of Amphor.

'Ask your question and hurry,' advised Yola nervously, who was now impatient to get away from this place before the terrible Guardian located them. He stood a little nearer to the edge of the Well and gazed down the shaft. Remembering the instructions of Ina, he spoke aloud.

'Spirit of the Well of Amphor, hear my question and grant me an answer so that I may act accordingly.'

From deep within the Well he was amazed to hear his own voice reply.

'Speak but ask one question only, for each may receive but one answer according to the law.'

Then Jeron replied to the voice. 'Tell me how may we journey to the world that I originally came from?'

They waited eagerly for the voice to reply. There was a moment's silence and then the devastating reply came.

'Such knowledge is forbidden by those who built this altar and gave a voice to the Well. Still, know this, since an answer of sorts must be given. Neither of you will ever make such a journey. For one of you it is impossible, and the other would not wish to go alone. Listen well to the voice within the Well of Amphor. In ages gone by there were those who travelled to the stars, using forbidden methods which, because they lacked a complete understanding, led to ultimate annihilation of their race. As they attempted to travel even further away to reach the tiny planets beyond the stars, an unexpected limitation was discovered. Those who proceeded beyond a certain distance were never seen again, because of a sudden change in phase which occurred in the relationship between successive events

100

in time. The accustomed continuity of time altered abruptly. When the return journey home was attempted it was discovered that the time required bore no relation to the relatively short outward journey. The alteration in synchronisation had added not just months, or even a year, to the time of the return journey, but centuries of time. Thus those who passed the critical point never saw their homes again, since once established, time is irreversible. The same phenomenon happens to those who like yourself have come to this globe from the star planets. Return to your world is impossible. You would age a thousand years before even half your journey had been completed. Thus your question has been answered.'

They looked at each other in great consternation. What could they do? At any moment the Guardian might appear. Tiros and his soldiers were waiting outside for them. Serainis was seeking for them in her own mind-reaching way. Now their one chance of complete escape was gone. Was there another, wondered Jeron as he racked his brains for a solution to the problem. He had a flash of inspiration. After all, Yola could still ask a question of the Well. He spoke to her urgently.

'It seems there is no escape that way, my dear, but although I have asked and received an answer, you have yet to ask one of the Well. Somehow we must use it to find a way of escape from Tiros and his men, and the thing that guards the Tomb.'

'Very well,' Yola replied sympathetically, 'but I think it is a great pity that you cannot see your world again, for I fear that this one is not so hospitable to live in, especially under these circumstances.' She went over to the Well of Amphor and leant over the edge of the surrounding rock. 'Tell me spirit who can answer all problems, how is escape possible from this place, avoiding harm from both that which guards the Tomb, and Tiros and his soldiers?'

Like Jeron, she was startled to hear her own voice coming up from the depths below.

'Leave as you have entered and none shall harm you. Thus your question is answered. Now leave this sacred place and visit it not again.' Then there was complete silence.

They left the small enclosure where the Well was situated and crossed the vast space of the Tomb. The giant twins stood there in frightening solemnity as below them the two humans crept past. When they arrived at the space in the passage-way where the Guardian had slept they edged along the opposite wall, but suddenly realised with sinking hearts that the nightmare being was no longer there. Remembering how silently and quickly it had moved despite the huge size of its body, Jeron strained his ears for an indication of its presence in the vicinity, but they heard nothing apart from their own breathing and the incessant dripping of water down the slimy sides of the passage. Further along the light increased slightly as they drew nearer to the exit point from the tunnel. Yola clutched his arm tightly.

'Look over there.' She pointed to a spot further along. Against the side of the passage something stood waiting silently. They drew cautiously nearer. Jeron fervently hoped that the prediction made about their escape was correct. Yola whispered in his ear, 'It's Tiros. I can see him now more clearly.' Her hair brushed against the sides of his cheek.

'Well, there's only him around as far as I can see. Let's advance and see whether my sword is better than his. We may have the advantage of surprise if he doesn't hear us too soon.'

He crept nearer to Tiros who stood with his back to Jeron. Something odd in the way the man stood struck Jeron, and beads of perspiration began to gather on his forehead. When he was close behind his adversary Jeron raised his sword, and taking hold of the man's shoulder, swung him around. He shrieked in horror, dropping his sword. Where the man's face had been, there was now a ghastly, yawning hole. The body collapsed with the movement and sank to the ground, like a rag-doll without the stuffing. Yola screamed madly as she came up to the sight. All need for caution was forgotten now as Jeron seized her hand and they ran from the awful heap that had once been human and alive. Into the entrance chamber they fled.

Something large and black lay on the floor, wheezing in its gluttoned sleep. There was a pervading smell of blood everywhere. They rushed past the nightmare and ran out into the clean air of the countryside. It took them several minutes to get their breath back. Jeron suddenly wondered where the soldiers had got to, but as he raised his eyes he saw on the opposite slope of grass the troop of uniformed men sitting round the remains of a fire. They sat very still. He paled visibly in the sunlight and taking Yola by the hand, gently led her away in the opposite direction. She wept for a long time. After a while they managed to find the place where they had left their horses, and thankfully rode off away from that place of silent death.

CHAPTER NINE

They were encamped in a small wooded area and had just finished the meagre remains of their food supplies. No fire had been lit for fear of arousing unwelcome interest from local inhabitants of the place, and so they were cold as well as being tired from their journeying.

'This is all very well,' said Jeron, rubbing his fingers as he tried to get some feeling back into his hands, 'but we can't keep this travelling up indefinitely. We must have some proper plan of where to go rather than just riding on to evade Serainis and her troops.'

Yola lifted her weary head and spoke back in sad tones. 'There is no one we can trust in these parts and it seems to me that only a matter of time separates us from Serainis. However far we go she will never call off the hunt, for it is her nature to persevere unceasingly until her purposes are accomplished. She probably does not know that you personally cannot show her the way to your world, so you represent to her a prize which would enable her power to increase enormously. Indeed she may not accept that you lack the knowledge she seeks, for depend upon it, she must be aware that you consulted the Well of Amphor and received an answer. I think that . . .' She broke off her conversation as the ring on Jeron's finger caught her gaze. It was no longer a dull red, metallic colour, but was now visibly becoming brighter with every second. Jeron followed her look of amazement and noticed the iridescent aura emanating from the glowing band of metal. A gentle warmth spread slowly from his hand to the rest of his body, reviving the tired muscles. His mind became refreshed and his thoughts clarified so that now all sorts of possibilities presented themselves.

'This is wonderful. I feel not just rejuvenated but fit to tackle any job however arduous.' He stopped for an instant, seeing how exhausted she was, and taking off the ring, gave it to her. 'Here, put it on and see how well you will feel. The energy of the ring seems to transfer itself to the wearer.'

She slipped the metal band on and received the same glow of soothing warmth that he had experienced. Within a minute she felt vibrant with energy and gave it back to him. She laughed. 'It's a pity we couldn't let the horses wear it, for then there would be little need for such long rests.'

He stared at her lovely face with those smiling mauve eyes, glowing lips and the glorious coppery hair, and knew that he loved her with an emotion far beyond anything he had ever felt before. She looked back at him and understanding his mood, took both his hands in hers and whispered softly to him. 'Be careful, man from another world, lest your purposeful gaze upon this maiden's face awaken a mutual response in her, and our friendly respect for one another gives way to a much stronger emotion. Whether it is the property of the ring or your own influence, I am not sure, but self-control could be readily lost unless some effort is made to maintain convention.' However, instead of retreating from him, he noticed that she drew a step closer, and the grasp upon his hands did not weaken. He bent down and kissed those hands so small inside his own, and seeing that she did not object to this, put his long arms around her tiny waist.

'Convention, my dearest, is a useful guide for behaviour when in the company of others, but here we are alone, and indeed we have been more than patient in this respect. Even so, there is a limit beyond which the endurance of love cannot reasonably be expected to be maintained.'

She started to protest, but he silenced those inviting lips in the most effective way possible, whilst he held her body taut against his. He murmured in her ear. 'Who knows what the future may hold for us? Surely we may not be damned for taking this brief moment of happiness as countless lovers have in times gone by. If you can deny that your thoughts and feelings are any less than mine then let us ride on to resume our dusty journey, but if, as I hope, you will not contradict me, then let us enjoy the happiness that is the right of all living beings.'

She looked up at him and trembled a little, but then as he waited with pounding heart she sighed and he saw that a suspicion of a smile blossomed upon her delightful features. Jeron pulled her arms around him and kissed her lips again with a savage hunger. She put her arms up around his neck and responded with equal passion. He lifted her up and she was taken further within the wood to a place where the green carpet of moss grew thickly and the sky above was hidden by the sheltering trees. A small stream meandered through the glade and as their love-making grew more wild they stripped off their dusty clothes in abandon and splashed each other with the cold water from the brook. Their laughter carried through the trees to where the horses stood, grazing on the lush grass.

Zaduk the Deviant frowned and motioned his men to where the sound came from. A monstrosity was Zaduk, blighted in his evil youth by some awful experiment which people could only guess at, for it was forbidden to talk of such a thing, the penalty being death. His head was uneven in shape, for the skull had atrophied on one side only, and the left eye had disappeared into the ridges of flesh. The arms were extremely long in proportion to the rest of the body, and were immensely strong. Few dared to cross swords with the Deviant for the strength and the long reach quickly despatched any who were so rash as to confront him with a challenge. But the abnormality of the body was nothing compared with the malignancy of the mind, and the screams of his prisoners reflected his insane practices. It was far better to kill oneself than to be taken alive by his followers.

Occasionally it would please him to go further afield than the regions of his own lands, and spy upon the camp of the Regent Tokin some miles distant from this border land. Now his quick ears had caught the playful laughter from the woods and he smiled broadly, for it seemed that good fortune had followed his expedition that day. Silently he followed his men into the trees as they spread out into a half-circle.

Lying upon him, she moved in ecstasy as the climax was reached, her finger-nails unknowingly scoring angry red scratches on his shoulders. Her sweet breath reached him in short gasps as his strong hands moved slowly down the arch of her naked back, curved over the pink mound of her thighs and caressed her. The ring on his finger was now no longer alive with magic.

The captain started to advance, but Zaduk stopped him with a signal. They were in no hurry. It pleased him to think how near they were and yet undetected by their prey. Decidedly, hunting human quarry was vastly superior to stalking the animal kingdom, although these, it was true, would be allowed little chance of running.

It was over now, and the great surge of sensual emotion had given way to a relaxed contentment. They lay there on the velvety moss, half-dreaming in a world of happiness. The soldiers crept forward, Zaduk at their head. Suddenly, Yola with a sickening feeling realised that they were not alone. She raised herself from his chest and looked around. Jeron lifted his head and was horrified to see a semi-circle formation of armed men before them. The two lovers scrambled to their feet. Yola ran to where their scattered clothes lay, but a caricature of a devil arrived there before her. He bowed to her and stretched forth his long, spindly, spidery arms.

'Why, lads, see what we have here. A nymph of the woods at the very least. Such are mentioned in the great Book of Fabled Creatures. Yes there is no doubt of this, for does she not display all the necessary characteristics?' His men roared with laughter at this and began to follow suit in their remarks. Jeron took her hand and advanced towards Zaduk.

'Stand away,' he said sternly. 'We have done you no harm. Shame on you to mock a maiden in such fashion. Move away and let us dress for the sake of modesty.'

Zaduk shook with convulsive laughter when he heard these words. 'What,' he spluttered, his eye rolling as he shook his head, 'did I hear right? Did you call this beauty here a veritable maiden? Surely not, for did not the very act we so innocently came across deny that description? No, no, my friend, you are deceived. This is indeed a nymph of the wood and must be treated so. In fact how am I to know that you are not a mythical being of the woods also. Come, my friends, Zaduk is not so ungenerous as you shall discover. You shall be my guests tonight for it is time to return to my humble abode, and my dear wife Keyla will be most pleased to entertain you.'

Despite their protests and efforts to struggle free their hands were tied behind their backs. Whilst Yola rode with Zaduk, Jeron's hands were tied to one of the Deviant's stirrups, so that he was forced to run by the side of the horse. Soon his feet were suffering from numerous cuts as the sharp flints caught the soles. The journey was a nightmare and Yola wished that she could faint to blot out the shame of her nakedness before the present company, but no merciful oblivion came to her. The ropes cut into her wrists, and the sight of her lover suffering on the road beside her caused unimaginable anguish.

Eventually their destination was reached and they were led over a drawbridge surmounting a wide moat into a castle courtyàrd. They were pushed·down innumerable steps which terminated· in a small passageway, barely greater than the height of· their guards. On either side of this passage were iron-barred cells and the two prisoners were separated so that they were in cells opposite each other. Both were chained to the wall, their arms being stretched above their heads, and then the guards left them after each in turn had spoken with relish of the possible fates which Zaduk might have in store for them. When these ruffians had gone the two captives spoke tenderly to each other, trying to get some comfort from such encouragement, but there was little to say and nothing to expect in the way of mercy. The ring on Jeron's finger was quite cold and no energy could be expected from that unpredictable thing. The pain from his feet was subsiding somewhat, but now a kind of numbness was creeping over his arms as the blood drained down into his body. Yola shivered with the cold of the stone wall against her slender back. Like Jeron her arms had lost most of their feeling and she began to wonder just how long they could survive under such conditions. Then she remembered that the captain had remarked to one of the guards that the guests of the Deviant only stayed here one or two nights at the most, no doubt before they expired. After a while she saw that Jeron being exhausted from the enforced run had dropped into unconsciousness, his head drooping forward on his chest. Her mind went round in circles as she thought about their plight, but she reflected that there was no way to bring help. Then she opened her eyes wide as her train of thought led to a spark of hope. There was only one person she knew who was even now looking for them and who might have the power to recognise their situation if Yola tried to get in mental touch. It was true that then they were delivering themselves to the very person they had been fleeing from, but at least it might buy them more time for survival, for the alternative was death by some cruel means within the day if she did nothing.

'Jeron, my love,' she cried to him, but he remained deep asleep in the opposite cell. At any moment Zaduk might return, but still she hesitated, for to act without telling Jeron seemed a denial of his trust in her. She spoke his name again, but still there was no response. It was no use, she would have to try to communicate with Serainis if she could.

Her eyes closed and she tried to blot out her surroundings and imagine a sheet of darkness in front of her. The images of Jeron and her cell persisted and interfered with her attempts to obliterate them. Iron bars danced before her eyes and an image of Zaduk stared at her with his one visible eye in that terrible asymmetric head, causing her to shake with fright. She drew in several deep breaths to steady herself. This was going to be much harder than she had realised. Furthermore, if Zaduk, who was within this castle, could also use the power of the mind, there was a strong danger of awakening his thoughts if his image kept creeping before her. Her arms ached badly and her right foot was beginning to itch unbearably. She opened her eyes and looked down. A large black rat was sniffing at her toes. She screamed in a frenzy of terror. Jeron lifted his head and peered across at her cell. There was a sound of footsteps on the stairs leading to the passage. The soldier captain walked up and looked at her with an appreciative eye.

'Well, wood nymph, as our master calls you, why do you sing so loudly?' He grinned as she blushed with acute embarrassment whilst he swept his admiring glance over her. She told him of the rat, which by now had vanished from sight.

'Rats, eh, well that's no surprise to me nor should you let it worry you, for to be eaten alive by one of those hungry beasts may well be considered a delicate treat compared with some of the ways our lady guests have been treated. Indeed, a body like yours creates a thousand new entertainments in the fertile imagination of Lord Zaduk.' He laughed as she paled visibly, and then casting a significant glance at silent Jeron, he left them alone again.

As soon as he had gone, Yola told Jeron of her plan to contact Serainis if she could. He agreed with her that their immediate salvation from these torturers was the priority and that perhaps they could escape from Serainis later on. Yola once more attempted the task, but now the picture of the rat presented itself all the time, and this preyed upon her nerves so much that she often had to open her eyes in order to satisfy herself of the rodent's absence. She gave up the attempt and suggested that Jeron try instead. He followed her instructions and managed to blot out his surroundings. Then he thought of Serainis and tried to give as much detail to the image as he could remember. Soon his mind was completely absorbed in his study of the enchantress. Her strikingly beautiful face stood before him in his mind and her green eyes looked back at him unblinkingly. Nothing happened and feeling greatly disappointed he told Yola. She thought for a while and then told him to imagine Serainis when she had entered into his mind. Of course, he thought, her eyes had then enlarged somehow so that they were all he had been aware of during that frightening time. He started again but now concentrated entirely upon her commanding, hypnotic eyes. He imagined them becoming larger as they had done once before, and he called her name out aloud. 'Serainis,' he cried, 'Serainis hear me.' Suddenly the image of the glittering green eyes altered. The pupils grew larger and without warning his brain became cramped with an increasing pressure. His body dangled at the end of the iron wrist chains as his last remaining strength was drawn from him. Again he became afraid at the supreme power emanating from behind the emerald eyes. She would kill him if his strength was drawn away at this intensity. He began to lose consciousness as points of light danced inside his brain. Questions probed his mind relentlessly. Answers were given but what transpired in this mental conversation he could not actively comprehend. He made an attempt to indicate the desperate urgency of their situation and the danger from Zaduk, but his fumbling mental pictures were impatiently snatched up and consumed as soon as he created them. Then he felt relief as the pressure was withdrawn and he knew that the audience was over.

He became aware once more of his grim surroundings and the pain of his body. Yola's naked form also sagged as her thin legs lost their supporting strength. The long mane of red hair cascaded over her white shoulders and hid her face from his eyes. He called her name softly as she lifted her tired head, he told her how the message of their plight had gone out to Serainis. She smiled thankfully, but was too exhausted to speak back. He wondered whether the beautiful sorceress would be able to stop Zaduk before any harm came to them. This castle had looked very secure from the outside and well guarded by the Deviant's followers. He noticed that Yola had fallen into a trance-like sleep again, and he was pleased to see that she at least could get some temporary relief in that way.

Steps sounded in the passage-way and Zaduk appeared with a company of richly dressed men and women. A well-built woman with long blonde hair and a bold face stood by the side of the Deviant, who introduced her.

'Greetings, my guests! This is Keyla who I promised would entertain you. Keyla, my dear, this is the wood nymph that I spoke of, and here is her male attendant.'

The blonde regarded Yola with a thoughtful smile and then she turned to appraise Jeron. Her eyes swept over his nude body with keen interest and she looked approvingly back at her husband. Zaduk spoke to Jeron.

'A few words of explanation are due to my guests. My dear

112

wife suffered a most unfortunate accident once with a sharp knife which I was holding at the time, and so regrettably is unable to speak to you herself, due to the lack of a tongue which became severed from its roots. She wishes me to say that she considers you are most excellent company for her tonight and she will personally entertain you both. Since she is an expert in such matters she feels that individual attention is better than amusing both of you at the same time, so the young lady will have to be patient and just observe, whilst you my friend are given your treat first. I trust you will find that Keyla will forget nothing in the lavish and exquisite entertainment she provides.'

The people gathered around him laughed heartily as he said this and crowded around the cell to watch as Keyla entered Jeron's cell. Yola was brought into the cell as well by two of the women and held so that she was forced to look on. Keyla stood before Jeron and looked at him for a considerable time, assessing his capabilities. Then she drank deeply from a wine cup provided by a smiling Zaduk, and took in a few long, deep breaths, as a tense state of fevered excitement stole over the onlookers. From the folds of her dress she drew a small knife with a curved, wicked blade, and staring into Jeron's eyes, tested the sharpness by placing the edge on one of her thumbs. A tiny scarlet bead formed and she held out her hand, letting the drop roll down the centre of his chest. He blanched, knowing that something dreadful was about to happen. Yola regarded the scene with horror. Keyla unwound her long, blonde tresses of hair and drew these slowly across his face, making his skin prickle with the contact. She drank some more wine and having drained the cup, placed it down on the floor between his chained feet. Her long pointed nails touched his shoulders lightly and caressed his muscles. He stared back at her with utmost loathing. There was nothing he could do to prevent her from touching him. The audience of people around the cell looked at him with inhuman eyes without pity. They drank in the scene with minds thirsting for something yet to come, something which he did not know about, but which they had witnessed many times before.

Zaduk's wife stepped closer to him. Silently she laughed, the woman without a tongue, her eyes fixed upon his as she brought her free hand down upon his chest. Keyla leaned forward an inch and kissed his resisting lips. Her hand descended to his bare stomach. There was complete silence as the men and women looking on caught their breath. Keyla smiled and her lips parted to show the sharp pointed teeth within. A pink stub of flesh at the back of her throat made a clicking noise as her hand descended lower. Jeron's naked body arched in reflex as she held him firmly. The light caught and sparkled on the blade as her other hand brought up the little razor-sharp instrument. Yola screamed and struggled violently with those who held her. Keyla waited with knife poised and looked away from Jeron to her husband. Zaduk waited until Yola was again held firmly, and then he smiled. He nodded and Keyla began to slowly draw the blade across. Pain swept through his body as a thin surface cut was made. Yola screamed again and then fainted. His vision swam and his legs tottered for a moment and then he recovered. Keyla was drinking from the cup, her face twisting as if in a kind of fit. Blood trickled down from the sides of her mouth. He realised with horror that it was his blood. His legs felt warm and sticky. She put the cup down in the same position and wiped her scarlet mouth with the back of her arm. She began again. This time he screamed in agony as the blade bit deeper. Blood dripped and spurted into the wine cup. His screams echoed along the passage-way and were heard by those descending the steps. The door was flung open and Serainis entered. Her eyes surveyed the scene angrily. Jeron saw her as if through a red mist, and then merciful darkness swept over him.

114

CHAPTER TEN

He was lying on a fur-covered couch, his body relaxed beneath a silk sheet after his long sleep, and warm from the heat of the room. How long had he slept like this? Recollection came of the last few moments before oblivion had swept over him. He discovered that now he had no pain from the ministrations of Keyla and sweat broke out on his brow as he tried to lift his head up from the couch. His brain reeled crazily with the effort and he found that he could hardly move. Mists gathered before his eyes and he yielded before them. When at last they had dispersed he tried to take further note of his surroundings without lifting his head. The room was richly decorated with walls bearing ornate scenes from mythology, and there hung fine carpets woven by master craftsmen. Carved marble columns reached up to the roof and the floor was tiled with thousands of tiny polished stones which reflected the light. At the side bowls of fruit and sweetmeats stood on a low onyx table and a heavy scent of flowers pervaded the atmosphere from a potted shrub bearing long glossy leaves. He noticed that his skin was now quite clean and had been bathed with some aromatic oil which left a sheen on the surface. There was no sign of Yola. Still at least these surroundings spoke of a desire to please and no doubt she was housed somewhere equally luxurious within these walls. He tried again to lift his head, somewhat more slowly this time, but it was no use. He was weaker than a baby.

An entrance curtain flapped open and Serainis in a long, silver dress stood at the foot of the couch, regarding him with a slight smile. She came nearer and pulled down the long silk sheet that covered his naked body. He attempted to move yet again, but sank quickly back as faintness overtook him. Serainis ignored his attempts at movement and examined the wound.

'Rest awhile, foolish man. Your anxiety regarding convention comes rather late, for you will recall that I saw you in similar state when your mind sought mine, and indeed during these last eight days I have personally cared for you, for is this not my own room?' She swept her hand around the place. Jeron was amazed.

'Then I have been here for that long?'

'Of course. Following the wounds inflicted upon you, I was hardly likely to raise from your state of unconsciousness to a painful awareness. In addition a general fever developed, which if it had been allowed to take its course, would have fatally consumed you. This necessitated providing you with a regimen of strong drugs, and when the fever had abated I considered it better that you remain drugged for the period of time needed for healing to take place. Apart from some interesting scars you are now as complete as before, I assure you.' She laughed at his obvious embarrassment, pulled the sheet up over his chest, and sat down on the side of his couch.

'What happened after I passed out?' he asked as he tried to gather his wits. 'Where is Yola?'

She ignored the first question. 'Our friend is resting not far from here. Indeed she suffered more than you, for whilst your injuries were painfully physical, hers were of the mind, and the latter are always slower to heal. Soon she will come to you.' Her perfume stole over him, subtly distracting his thoughts. With an effort he persisted with his line of questioning.

'How did you persuade Zaduk to give us up?'

She frowned and brushed aside a wandering strand of black hair from her forehead. 'I doubt whether you will like the answer much, but if you insist I will tell you.' She raised her

116

wide eyebrows. He nodded his head, so she continued.

'I promised Zaduk that after I had extracted what I wanted from you for my purpose, he could have you back.'

He froze. She listened to his thoughts as his hands clenched in fear and anger, and then she stood up and said to him coldly, 'You insult me with your thoughts and looks of rage. Do you imagine that I would be so cruel in reality to give you both back to the very fate from which I rescued you? Truly you know little enough of me and my moods.' She turned to go, but he spoke heatedly back to her despite his weakness.

'How could I believe otherwise? Your previous dealings with us left little to be desired. I have not forgotten how my body was manipulated for your murderous designs on Yola and myself. Is that the act of a merciful person? Do you deny that you sent Tiros after us with your troops to slaughter us?' He sank back exhausted.

Serainis turned slowly around and stared hard at him. 'What talk is this,' she said, 'of murder and violence? Of course I sent Tiros after you when it became known that you had left the instructed route I sent you on, and accordingly he was asked to seek you out as a friend. When his men arose from their camp to greet you, they were surprised to see Yola fleeing from them, and you bearing down upon them with a sword in your hand. Not unnaturally they defended themselves from your unprovoked attack. These things I know, for I was in mind contact with Tiros all the while. As for the Dead Forest, it is well known that unusually strong influences still exist there and it is therefore no surprise to me that you behaved abnormally. I begin to think that perhaps it would have suited you better to have been left in the sharp embrace of fair Keyla.'

Confused, he did not know what to think. He remembered how she had shown him that he was the agent of dead Pandilex, and so opposed to her. He had been set in a trance in which she had tried to make him kill Yola and himself. There was no doubt in his mind about this and yet what was the point in her denying this? On the other hand he had assumed that they would remain as her prisoners once they were free from Zaduk, but this room was her own and clearly no prison. Certainly Tiros had initially greeted them as a friend, but had soon led them to an ambush. Serainis broke through his conjecture.

'So that is what you thought had happened. The strange powers of the Dead Forest seemed to have warped your memory and your judgement. Perhaps Yola has been less affected in this way. Let us see if she can throw some light on this problem.' She went out of the room and returned with Yola, who looked rather pale, but greeted him with gentle affection and much concern. He assured her that he had been well looked after, and said graciously that he was in the best of hands. Serainis gave him a kinder look when he said this, and some of the tension between them evaporated. They chatted about what had happened, but it seemed to Jeron that a lot was left unsaid. Yola appeared to be cautious in the presence of Serainis, which perhaps was the wisest thing to do. She agreed that although it seemed like an ambush at the time, the soldiers may have misinterpreted Jeron's drawn sword and her abrupt exit as a threat upon themselves. Serainis explained that Tiros had followed them into the cave in order to find them and warn them of the dangers there. Jeron was now both confused and suspicious, but conceded to himself that at least they had been fortunate in escaping from Zaduk and his evil wife, and his present circumstances were definitely preferable. One could not deny that Serainis had saved their lives. He apologised to Serainis for his ungrateful manner and thanked her for her timely intervention.

Serainis smiled a little wistfully. 'No, Jeron, I do not want either apologies or praises, only a sincere and lasting friendship, with a mutual regard born from absolute trust. Believe me when I say that although even now you still have doubts and uncertainties, there will come a time when the contagious spell of the Dead Forest will lift from your mind, and you will see again more clearly. Meanwhile give us the benefit of your doubt and trust in us, for you behold two friends before you who have your best interests at the centres of their hearts.' She took Yola's hand and the two women left the room after Yola had promised to see him the next day. He felt terribly tired and the effort of thinking was almost too much to bear, so he allowed himself to drift into a dreamless sleep.

In the evening Serainis appeared with a phial of blue liquid and pouring the contents into a cup of wine, made him drink the bitter liquid. She was very lovely, her silky, black hair being drawn up high upon her forehead and kept in position with a gold circlet. The blue robe suited her well. When he had finished drinking, she leaned forward and took the cup from him. The contact of her thin fingers upon his hand made him tremble in some inexplicable way.

'No longer will you be sleepy from my drugs, for this I have given you will clear the mind and refresh the body. Tomorrow you can get up and strengthen your legs with walking and exercise. Soon you will be as before, or even better. However, I see that there still exists some doubt as to your condition. Do not deny this, for all that is written in your mind may be seen as clearly as you can view the lines on your hands. Because of this doubt which makes you fear your own ability, and causes you to dread your reunion with the one you love, I shall send to you this night proof that your worries of manly shame are needless. This I do so that you may learn to trust me further without cause for suspicion, for know this, Jeron, I have much need of true and loyal followers, but those who hesitate to take the hand of my friendship I reject forever.' She left him wondering at her words, and at the softness of her tone which was so in contrast with the ice-cold manner he was used to hearing. She was certainly a woman of contrasting moods. They had given themselves back to her expecting to be dealt with as her prisoners, and instead were being treated as favoured guests.

The evening was warm, but a faint breeze stirred the curtains in the room and he lay there relaxed and content. The liquid he had been given had suffused throughout his body and filled him with a sense of well-being. For a short while he slept and then awoke on hearing a slight noise. He opened his eyes cautiously. Someone stood at the side of the couch. He recognised the perfume as the peculiar subtle fragrance stole over him. She stood there with a faint smile on that face of ethereal beauty, a thin cape of pure white fur wrapped around her. She stood there, not moving, as if turned to stone. She was like a carved, ivory statue, a goddess depicting all in womanhood that man had ever desired. A minute passed and still she did not move, but the smile remained there, enigmatic and enthralling, as the emerald eyes reached deeply into his. He dared not say anything lest the vision disappear from his sight. Was it indeed Serainis or some strange dream of his? An awful thought crossed his mind that here was something with no life at all, some horror from beyond the grave, come to claim him in the night. He began to tremble and sweat as the beautiful being stayed there motionless beside him, her eyes upon his, the haunting smile on her ivory face.

He could bear the suspense no longer. His hand reached out in a nervous jerk and touched the fur cape. The covering slid slowly down to the ground and he caught his breath as all her white nakedness was revealed to his eager sight. His heart leapt with sensual desire. Jeron put out his trembling hand and touched her ice-cold fingers. He almost shrieked when they closed about his. She laughed silently. She was no Goddess of Death. She was Life itself. He reached up and kissed her, his nude body tense with excitement. They caressed each other and she stroked his head softly as he bent down over her as she lay on the couch. He kissed the scarlet nipples erect on the rounded breasts. Gone was all the suspicion and fear that he had harboured in the past. Now he worshipped her in a way that he could never act with Yola. This siren knew too much about him, the way he thought, the delights to his senses that even now he was discovering with her embraces. She made love to him with an abandon which more than satisfied the violent urges of passion aroused in his body by her magnificent beauty. Almost before he realised it himself, the changes in his desire were anticipated each time, keeping him continually riding on a tidal wave of sensual ecstasy, teasing him, pleasing him, frustrating and dominating his desire until all the passion had flooded from him. Then they slept with each other for a while, and later made love again, and yet again. Finally, their need of each other satiated completely, they slept, their arms twined about each other as if inseparable, her head on his chest, her silky hair over his face. Throughout the night no words had been said, for the language of love needed no utterance. Curiously he shivered in his sleep, for the heat from his body did not compensate for the icy temperature of the lovely one within his embrace.

As they lay there on the couch the entrance curtain moved silently and Serainis stood there regarding the scene. Then she whispered certain words in the ear of the sexual toy in Jeron's arms. The woman gently disentangled herself from his clasp, silently arose from the couch, and knelt with humility before her mistress. Then Serainis touched the face so like her own, making a sign upon the forehead, whereupon a remarkable series of changes occurred and after a minute the original features returned. They left Jeron sleeping the dream of his illusion, Serainis going out of the castle to walk in the moonlight, and Ginah returning to her rooms.

In the morning he awoke but only the perfume lingered in the air around him. He arose and put on the new set of clothes left on the table beside him. The memory of the night haunted him, and he longed to see Serainis but he was told by one of her servants that she had left the castle early that day and would not be back before sunset. He wandered around the gaunt castle and after a little while managed to locate Yola. She was sitting before a small mirror tying her coppery hair into place as he entered the room, and she turned around with evident pleasure to greet him. They embraced each other and exchanged news, although naturally enough he did not speak of the night before. Inwardly he cursed himself as pangs of conscience stabbed at him for his infidelity. The strange powers and wild beauty of Serainis were unmatchable, but the fresh loveliness and true honesty of Yola brought forth his real love.

The two of them walked through the castle and found a pleasant little flower garden tucked away within the outer walls. Here they sat on the grass and passed the time in idle conversation away from the rest of the inhabitants of the fortress. The talk soon turned to the mystery of Serainis.

'The trouble with Serainis is that no one knows exactly what does go on in her mind,' declared Yola, mischievously pulling the petals off a daisy. 'Apparently we are now accepted back in her favour, though I find her replies to my questions somewhat disconcerting in their obliqueness, and this leads me to conclude that we are not trusted quite as much as she lets us believe. Her explanations regarding the murderous attack on me, and Tiros's ambush, lack sincerity. Tiros was our good friend until we last saw him alive, so what could have changed him so dreadfully? Sometimes I wonder whether Serainis ever fully recovered from her earlier experiences in life, for when she was younger and Syndra was alive, she was a much happier and less complicated person in many respects.'

Jeron sat up, interested in this aspect of their conversation. 'You think that she changed mentally for some reason earlier on in her life? When was this?'

'After her father had put Syndra to death, Serainis disappeared, so it was said, because she could not live in the same place as her father.' She threw the denuded flower away and picked another one from the grass.

'This is very interesting. Why was her sister put to death by old Pandilex?'

Yola laughed at him. 'You have scant respect it seems for the dead ruler of the South, who sent you here. Well, Syndra was the twin sister of Serainis, and although they were much alike in appearance, Syndra was considerably more advanced in the arts of sorcery, whereas Serainis studied less and enjoyed life more. However the two sisters were very devoted to each other, although as time passed their interests and personalities diverged considerably. There came a time when rumours started in the court that plots to overthrow Pandilex stemmed from one very close to him though no one dared mention names. Then one day notice was given that Syndra had been arrested following an abortive attempt to overpower Pandilex. The was put to death in the customary vile fashion reserved for assassins.'

'What was that?' He brushed away a fly that persistently flew around him.

'In the old part of Jevra there is a pit wherein lives a gigantic serpent. It has always been there as long as men can remember. Syndra was stripped, tied and lowered slowly down to be consumed by the reptile.'

'She must have suffered terribly before the end came. What a terrible way to have to die.'

'No, you are wrong there. She did not suffer at all.'

He looked unbelievingly at her. 'What, do you mean to tell

me all that happened to her and yet she felt nothing, surely not?'

Yola nodded her pretty head. 'Yes, for during the whole time she was being lowered to the serpent, she remained still and silent, looking ever upwards at the crowd above. Even when the end came the only sound that was heard came from the reptile.'

'That's unbelievable! She was conscious all the time you say and yet did not even flinch at the thought of what waited for her below.' She nodded again.

He sat back on the grass and thought about the scene which must have taken place. Yola continued. 'Before the end came Serainis pleaded with her father for the life of her sister, but the seer had given the order. When her twin died Serainis rushed from the place in obvious mental torment and was never seen by her father again, despite intensive searches subsequently. After Pandilex's long life finally ended, it became known that Serainis had taken over the derelict Quartz Castle and had it rebuilt in the parts where repairs were needed. She presented no legal claim for the lands of the South and these therefore fell to Raitis, the appointed successor to Pandilex.'

'I begin to see why Pandilex adopted the precaution of having Serainis investigated after his death, since he could not find her after Syndra's execution. No doubt he became suspicious of her too, for if he was capable of believing that one twin was evil enough to die, then the other must also have been under a cloud of suspicion. It seems to me that whether I like it or not, I am still obeying the will of Pandilex, for Serainis represents a mystery to me that must be solved.' He told Yola again of the way in which the sorceress had hypnotised him to attempt the murder of Yola. The two differing aspects of Serainis, her apparent evil acts against them and her subsequent attempts to regain their confidence, gave no grounds for trust. Yet was she predominantly evil as her sister had apparently been, or was there still some good remaining from the young girl that Yola had admired before the death of Syndra?

As he thought about this, an idea began to grow. If indeed Serainis genuinely knew nothing of her attempts to take their lives, then it was possible that she might be suffering from some sort of split personality. It was not inconceivable that the shock of seeing her twin sister die had caused a great disruption in her mental processes. Part of her would hate the murderer of her sister and the other part would desist from taking action against her father. Perhaps the deeds that she initiated in vengeance of her dead sister would not be consciously acceptable to the other side of her character. In this way she would exist as a dual personality, each part being ignorant of the other. What was the correct term? He screwed up his forehead trying to remember the word. It was no use, the memories from that previous world were rapidly being forgotten and perhaps it was better so. Yola received his idea without much conviction. He could see that she did not accept the idea in principle and so the subject was not pursued.

CHAPTER ELEVEN

Serainis returned late that night and they did not see her
until the next morning. She seemed somewhat distant in her
attitude towards them, although her words were friendly
enough. She indicated that the past mistrust between them
was forgotten and that they were welcomed back to her court
of admirers. This seemed the best solution for all, for as Jeron
observed, they would have no chance of escape this time if
they declared themselves opposed to her, since now they
were alone together only within the castle walls. They discovered this when one day they attempted to go horse riding
and found to their surprise that a company of riders accom-
panied them ostensibly for the purpose of protection from
Zaduk's roving marauders. After a short distance they were
turned back as it was considered too dangerous to stray far
from the fortress.

A few days later Serainis informed them that Zaduk had
surprisingly formed an alliance with the Regent Tokin, who
now could no longer be relied upon for safe conduct across
his lands. This, together with the death of Raitis, had served
to shift the balance of power even further to the edge of the
precipice of war. A general atmosphere of conspiracy pervaded
everywhere and Serainis ordered that additional fortifications
be made at the outer walls of the castle approaches. Jeron
being bored with little to do, helped in the erection of these
walls and in so doing got to know many of the soldiers. Once
when the ring he wore became hot, as it did now and then in
an unpredictable fashion, the strength it supplied allowed
Jeron to raise by himself a stone column, which several of his
fellows had been struggling with. This earned him an un-

justified reputation, but he was careful not to contradict them, since there was little point in indicating the strange powers of the ring when it might have been stolen for such magical properties.

At first he could not work out why the ring glowed and heated up at such odd times. It seemed to act as a power supply on these occasions and such power could be used in various ways. With a little practice he found that he could direct the energy if he concentrated hard enough. The power so provided also acted upon other people if he wished, and once he surprised Yola by rapidly healing an arm wound she sustained when her horse threw her to the ground. The more he used the forces supplied by the ring, the more it activated itself, until one day he realised that power flooded from the band of metal whenever he required it, and he knew then that he was master of the device. The potential power supplied was enormous and he had to be very careful not to arouse people's suspicions, so the feats he accomplished with it were carried out when no one else was present. He learnt how to adjust the intensity of force by regulating his own strength of will and it was comforting to know that he now possessed a weapon of his own far more dangerous than those held by the soldiers around him. Only Yola knew of his secret and advised him to keep it well guarded since it might easily be their only defence if they lost favour with Serainis.

One night they were leaving Serainis's apartments with her other guests after a pleasant evening of conversation when their hostess indicated to them to stay for a while. After the others had left she talked with them on trivial matters endeavouring to put them at their ease, but Jeron noticed that she was tense and excited. Intuitively he became suspicious regarding her motives for keeping them there and waited to see what she had in mind. The talk turned to politics and Serainis told them that the present situation was becoming increasingly difficult to maintain. The alliance between Tokin and Zaduk had brought a greater pressure to bear upon her forces and it seemed that soon outright war would be inevitable. In the struggle that would develop many people from both sides would perish. She told them how she had thought deeply trying to find an answer to this problem. If only she could concentrate all her forces on one of the enemy camps she was confident that the battle would be won, but now with the combined efforts of the opposing alliance turned against her, additional help was desperately needed. Yola and Jeron did not need to be reminded that they owed their lives to her efforts in deceiving Zaduk, nor normally would she have asked for their help in return. However this situation involved not only themselves, but all her followers, and as their leader she had a moral responsibility to obtain help in whatever way was possible. Jeron thought that this sounded vaguely like a threat. The next words came as no surprise to him. Serainis asked him whether it was possible to obtain help from the world that he had originated from. If he could but recall the words of power that Pandilex had taught him, then they could open the way back to his planet again.

He felt his heart beating strongly as he thought of his reply. He shook his head slowly and explained why it was no longer feasible. There were still many things that he did not remember. Though the reasons for his presence had been made clear enough, the events prior to his arrival on this planet refused to be recalled to his mind. Some indications of how life had been in that other world of his had been shown to him by Ina, the old witch of the Dead Forest, but the actual scene where he started his journey was lost forever. Neither her powers nor those belonging to Serainis had managed to identify the words of power he had used at that time.

Serainis's keen eyes flashed with anger and the knuckles of her hands whitened as they gripped the carved arms of her chair. 'Nothing is impossible,' she declared in chilling tones. 'I demand that you recall the words of power. Think hard and think deeply. The knowledge is still there, imprisoned within your being. We shall even yet seek it out and isolate it.' She craned forward towards him like some evil predator within sight of easy prey. He felt her will draining his resistance rapidly, but then remembered the ring. He drew upon the reserves of energy within the strange device. The effect upon Serainis was startling. She gave a loud cry as if a sword had struck her and fell backwards on to the carpeted floor. As she did so, a stream of shimmering light spilled forth from a point between her eyes and gathered shape beside her.

'Look,' cried Yola in horror, pointing with her forefinger, 'her spirit has left her body.'

The source of light twisted and moved as if in torment. As they watched, it split into two parts and these reformed into human-like shapes although rather faint and misty in appearance. The figures of light were not identical. One was less opaque than the other and bore a distinct resemblance to Serainis's body which lay a few feet away. It was the other ghostly figure, larger than life, which caused Yola to go white with fear and to grip Jeron's arm again. She pointed to the larger area of light which lay writhing slowly on the floor in front of them.

'Do you not understand? This thing bears the living resemblance of Syndra, the dead twin sister of Serainis. Yet how of all things can this be, for Syndra expired a long while ago? What frightful supernatural process have we initiated now?' She shivered and clung closely to the warmth of her lover's body. Jeron put his long arm around her and wondered whatever would happen next. He didn't have to wait long. As they watched, the visions merged together, spun round and so twisting, sank together into the body of Serainis. Soon Yola noticed that Serainis was breathing again more normally. They carried her inert body to a couch and laid her carefully on it.

'It seems that my hunch about her was right after all,' whispered Jeron into Yola's ear, 'although I did not expect her to be quite such a literal mixture of identities.'

She stared at him as the meaning of his words dawned upon her. 'If I understand you right, you mean that she is not really simply Serainis as I once knew her, but a living hybrid of both twin sisters.'

He shook his head impatiently. 'No, my dear, for if she were as you have described, then she would act in a more co-ordinated manner surely. However, we know that she does one thing and denies it subsequently. I think that the spirit of Syndra entered into the twin body of Serainis at the time of the serpent-pit drama, when Serainis's own mind and spirit were considerably disturbed. This would account for the quiet way in which Syndra met her death. In fact her own body was probably vacated before it was lowered to the serpent. I think that Serainis is ignorant of the fact that she acts as host to the twin soul of her dead sister. Acts caused by the soul of Syndra are concealed from her own true identity and so the unpredictable behaviour of Serainis is explained.' He stopped for an instant to listen to Serainis, but she was still uncon- scious. 'When Syndra or that which was Syndra's soul tried to make me reveal the words of power, I used the magic ring to oppose her. The sudden shock must have struck her by surprise and caused the strange phenomenon we saw.'

Yola regarded the inert body of Serainis sleeping on the couch. 'So at last we have solved the enigma of Serainis. Per- haps now that we can understand her problem we can some- how make her aware of it too, and stop these tendencies towards acts of evil.'

He frowned. 'I'm not sure whether that would be wise. She may not believe us, and in addition we apparently have no way of warning her of this condition without alerting that which also lives within her. Who knows what she might do under such circumstances? I think it is probably better that we pretend for the time being that nothing has happened.'

'No,' said Yola slowly, 'she will know the truth anyway for you forget you cannot conceal your thoughts from her. As soon as she awakes and reads your mind, she will be aware of what has happened. We must be honest with her and appeal to her to understand the situation. By the way, did you see the difference in size between the two astral spirits, and the denser appearance of Syndra's manifestation? It looks as if Syndra's soul has acted like a parasite feeding on the sister, for the differences are most noticeable.'

Jeron looked thoughtfully at Yola. 'I suppose that in time the spirit of Syndra will absorb all that is left of the soul of her twin.'

Yola was shocked at the suggestion. 'No, Jeron, we cannot allow this process to continue. Somehow we must drive out the invading soul from Serainis's body and allow the weakened spirit of the host to recover. Perhaps then one day we shall see Serainis in all her former glory as I remembered her years ago.'

He didn't share her enthusiasm. 'But how can one deal a blow to Syndra without equally affecting Serainis? If we are restricted in this way I just don't see how it can be accomplished. It might even be better to kill now that which sleeps upon the couch so that a lot of evil may perish at the expense of a little good. In order to kill Syndra it is necessary to murder Serainis.' Even as he said these words he blanched at Yola's expression. He wished that he hadn't spoken his thoughts aloud to her.

'Shame on you, Jeron, for I thought you were a man of honour and integrity. Did not the great Pandilex himself send you here on a mission to solve the mystery of Serainis and administer justice to her if necessary? You must comply with

131

this obligation or be subject to his vengeance from the grave. Who knows but that his dead eyes may be watching you even at this very moment?'

Icy needles ran down his spine when these words were uttered and he knew that there would be no rest for him until his formidable task was completed, although just how this was to be accomplished he wasn't sure. He was like a man skating on very thin ice. At any moment the present situation could develop into something acutely dangerous for both of them. They were dealing now with two unknown quantities, instead of one, both abnormal in their ability to control and bend the minds of mere mortals like Yola and himself. The atmosphere was full of potential menace to say the least.

The beautiful figure on the couch stirred and raised herself up. They looked at her as she opened her eyes wide at them. Who looks at me now, wondered Jeron, from behind those lovely eyes, Serainis or Syndra? Too late he realised with horror that his thought had been instantly read just as easily as if he had shouted the words aloud.

Her face became white with shock at the realisation that they knew the truth about her. For some moments she had difficulty in controlling her obvious emotion, but finally regained control of herself and when she spoke to them her voice was cool and silky.

'I greet you both now without the veil of illusion which it seems you have so cleverly penetrated. Do not look so fearful, dear Yola, for did you not know me once as the sister of Serainis? Yes, I am she whom you once called Syndra, who once was admired in the lands of the South and beyond as a woman of beauty and a sorceress of unparalleled knowledge. Even my father, curse his memory, with all his arts was unable to see through the trickery with which I evaded the terror of the serpent pit. He it was who sent you here, Jeron, to act as my judge and executioner. Well, now that you comprehend a little better the puzzle which he sent you to investigate, perhaps you will show the quality of understanding of which he was incapable. Kill me and you kill Serainis, for though diminished in strength, the flame of her spirit still flickers inside this body. Thus I sought and entered the one refuge which was inviolable to those who loved Serainis and so my unshielded spirit was protected from possibility of future attack.

'You fear for my sister? Such fears are groundless for contrary to your suspicions I love my sister as deeply as any could, for is she not the twin with whom I shared my mother's womb? When Serainis understood from her father that my murder was his intention, she died a thousand deaths anticipating what was to come. As she saw my final moments approach the agony proved too much for her and the flame of her spirit became weak. Without doubt she would have died within moments of my demise, unable to live on after the death of her twin. This I knew, for we were always mentally in tune with each other and especially so at that time. In this disturbed state her spirit began to ebb and I saw in that moment how escape from the torture to come was possible and how Serainis's life could also be saved. Too late I hesitated before saying those awful words of power which transferred the essence of my soul to the haven of her body. In those few seconds a terrible injury had been inflicted upon her and no longer was she the strong and bright spirit I had known. Powerful enchantments were desperately needed at once to heal her crippled soul, and I rushed her body from the serpent arena as my own vacated shell was lowered below.

'Months of patient effort have been rewarded by a slow but steady recovery. Serainis is still extremely weak and it is doubtful whether her full strength will ever return. Thus you behold us, twin spirits in one body, Syndra useless without her sister's body, Serainis's health dependent on her twin's sorcery. Jeron, you who are the agent of Pandilex, is it not time that you reconsidered your position in this affair? You have acted upon behalf of the murderer of my mother, who killed my body, and would have caused the death of Serainis. Use your keen intelligence, Jeron, and reason to yourself with that cold outworld logic of yours; which is the most injured party? Remember also that Pandilex is long since dead, crumbled to ashes, whilst I before you live on, strong in knowledge, powerful in sorcery. Would you destroy the beauty of Serainis, which as mine was once, is admired and desired by all men? Can you bring yourself to kill me, for remember that in doing so, you bring the shame of Serainis's murder upon your head?' She leaned back and poured some wine out into a cup, and drank deeply. Her mysterious eyes were very bright and contrasted with the pale beauty of her skin. He thought that she had never looked lovelier than at this moment but still the voice of doubt nagged in his brain. He had only her word that that was what had happened to Serainis. Supposing that Syndra had deliberately weakened Serainis's spirit, for Syndra was considerably more expert in magic than her twin who therefore could defend herself less easily. Certainly it was true that if he killed Syndra he would be murdering Serainis at the same time. He was not at all sure in any case that he could overcome the formidable strength opposed to him, even though he had the ring, he remembered. Yet if what she said was completely true then Syndra had been the salvation of Serainis and their undoubting loyalty was due to her. How could he know which version was the true one? Could she explain the murder attempt in the Dead Forest and the behaviour of Tiros?

She put her hand out and placed it lightly upon his. 'Yes, I will answer those questions though you have not voiced them.' She turned to Yola who had also been trying to read Jeron's thoughts but had failed to catch most of them. 'Jeron naturally still has doubts, for your experiences in the Dead Forest and the Tomb of the Twins are not easily forgotten. When you asked me about these matters last time I was unable to give you a true explanation, for the matter of my presence here is one that I do not wish to be known since there are still alive those who followed Pandilex and who would seek my destruction. My foremost duty is to protect Serainis who is not able to defend herself effectively. When it became known to me that you were an agent of my father I feared that somehow my secret was revealed. Forgive me, for I freely confess that I sent you on your way with murder instilled in your spellbound mind. It knew that if the old witch Ina discovered that you had murdered an innocent within her house you would have died in turn from the wrath of her justice. Thus neither death would have been attributable to me. When this failed, I sent Tiros with a company of soldiers after you, but the spirit of Serainis pleaded with me and I saw that my actions were wrong and unworthy of us. Therefore by incantation I stopped Tiros from advancing further to overtake you in the Tomb. Thus in turn he met his own ghastly death as did his troops by their inaction. The memory of their deaths haunts me yet, for I was so involved in mentally following you that for a vital time I lost my contact with them.'

She bowed her head as her shoulders moved in anguish. Yola was unable to bear the sight of such emotion in one who had always been so proud, and she took Serainis's hands and tried to comfort her. In a little while the latter raised her head and pushed back the long, jet-black hair.

'Jeron still says nothing. My appeal to him has gone in vain I think. What can I tell you that hasn't already been said? What further can one confess?'

Most people would have given up at that point, but despite Yola's glare of disapproval, he swallowed his embarrassment and ploughed on. 'Syndra, it appears that there has been much misunderstanding between us, but now it seems that we shall keep no further secrets from each other and therefore gain much in mutual trust. Thus it is that I respectfully maintain it is vitally necessary to eliminate all possible doubts that remain. I refer to the matter of Serainis herself. In the past when you spoke to us, no doubt we were replied to by yourself. I would therefore like to converse with Serainis in person, for she alone can verify for you the events of the recent past.'

Syndra thought for a moment in silence and then said, 'Very well, it shall be so. Realise though that I speak physically with the voice of Serainis also, so you will discern no change in sound. Still, to prevent any suggestion of trickery upon my part I will ask my sister to describe some past event where Yola, but not myself, was present. Therefore previous to this moment I would have no personal knowledge of this event where only Yola and my sister had been present. Thus you will be satisfied that it is indeed the spirit of Serainis that addresses you. I shall now remain silent until you ask for me by name, though I caution you to be gentle with my sister, for she tires easily.'

She stopped speaking and waited there, looking at them. This is incredible, thought Jeron. In a moment this woman will speak again and this time an entirely different personality will be directing the voice. How can they both exist in the same body without a complete take-over by one or the other? Well, if Yola could be convinced that Serainis was indeed a co-habitant by the demonstration of knowledge of events which Syndra could not have known about, then Serainis could tell them whether Syndra's story was true or false. Unfortunately, of course, this all assumed that Syndra exerted no unknown pressure upon her sister to reveal the information she lacked. He had a nasty feeling that the demonstration proved nothing either way.

Yola spoke. 'Greetings, dear Lady Serainis. Because of what has happened in recent events I must establish your identity

136

for my own satisfaction. I therefore ask you to recall some details for me of a time some years ago when we were both together but Syndra was absent.'

The silky voice spoke again, this time a little fainter and more hesitant. 'My dear Yola, my sister has told me what it is that you require and I shall endeavour to give you a satisfactory answer. The proof of this little exercise is not the description of events that you yourself now recall, for either twin could know your thoughts and repeat aloud the fancies therein. No, the demonstration of my identity beyond doubt is shown by reminding you of particulars associated with this event that you have forgotten until now, but which I still remember. Ask your question then and we shall see how keen our memories are.'

Yola thought deeply for a while and then made up her mind. 'A long time ago I met you for the very first time. When was this? What did I wear? Who was with me?'

'These are things which you recall and therefore both we twins have knowledge of. Our immediate replies thus prove nothing regarding the identity behind this voice, but I will answer all the same and then follow with the real proof you require.' She paused for a moment and then continued. 'I saw you first when you were a young child on a summer's eve. You wore the clothes traditional to your people who were with you on that occasion. These are facts of which we all have knowledge, but now recall these, which are not yet remembered by you. With you also was a small white dog that growled so fiercely at my noble horse. Your father wore a long leather tunic which was painted with designs of deer. Upon your right arm you wore a circlet of yellow metal cast in the shape of a fish biting its tail. Do you now remember?'

'Of course,' exclaimed Yola delightedly, 'my little dog Kiki upset your great stallion and so your attention was diverted away from my father to me. My father always wore his best tunic for important events and we were told that the Lady Serainis would stop at our village after hunting that day. The fish circlet was my only piece of jewellery and so naturally I wore that for the occasion. Oh, Jeron, this is indeed Serainis without doubt. Forgive me, my Lady, for ever having doubted.'

'Me too,' added Jeron hastily, 'but such a demonstration was necessary if all uncertainties were to be banished completely. Syndra's descriptions of the events which led up to her "execution" are therefore correct, are they not?'

'Yes, Jeron and Yola. My dear sister has kept my poor spirit alive all this time, through her encouragement and skill. I think that amends should be made to her for the suspicion in which she has been held, for our secret has not been the easiest to keep from such acute minds as yours and others. Now I must rest awhile for even such small efforts as these tire me considerably. My dear sister will converse with you again for the meanwhile.'

She lapsed into silence and once again Jeron found the whole business very weird. However Yola was convinced and so he accepted with resignation the success of the test of identity. Just how two spirits could live in one body he did not understand, but then there were so many things about this world that were mysterious. He looked over at the two women. Yola was speaking with Syndra presumably, who was a little cold in her approach now that their doubts about her had apparently been swept away. Both twins were apt to be variable in their moods Yola had told him once and he thought how true that observation was. He doubted whether anyone could ever truly be their friend, for like queens with their subjects, Syndra and Serainis kept the initiative on their side all the time. On the night he had lain in Serainis's room, he had, it appeared, made love to both sisters at once without realising it. Annoyance crept over his face and then all at once

138

he was struck by the humour of the situation and laughed aloud.

They stopped talking and glanced over in his direction.

'Sorry,' he said, 'I didn't mean to interrupt you. Please go on.' They resumed their conversation but he noticed that Syndra (or was it Serainis?) now had a curious gleam in her eyes. Really, he said to himself, not even these thoughts are private from her.

She gave him an amused glance as they all left the room. Let the fool cherish his illusions. No man had ever truly possessed her in a carnal sense. If the animal side of her nature was ever allowed to come to the surface, no normal man would be strong enough to withstand her violent emotions and retain his sanity. One day, perhaps, she would find a partner like herself, someone not quite human, a hybrid born of supernatural union between parents whose blood should never have mixed. One day, but meanwhile her would-be suitors unwittingly acted out their little charades with Ginah, for Ginah wearing the mask of Serainis, received her own rewards for loyal service to her mistress. Few men spared a glance for Ginah when the beauty of Serainis was there for all to be dazzled by. Yet this quiet girl who kept much in the background of Serainis's court, knew more of hidden passions and secret intrigues than anyone bar Serainis herself. This surrogate of love had spoken softly to her mistress about the strong, handsome man from the world beyond the stars, and for once, it seemed, had been allowed her own choice that night. However, few things happened unless they also suited Serainis, and so Ginah waited patiently for the time when Jeron would be alone with her again.

Taylor gasped as the sweat poured from him. This was terrible but the worst was yet to come. Soon there would be a time when his sweat glands would no longer extract water from his tissues. Then his internal temperature would slowly rise so that he would be in a torture of discomfort. His parched lips had begun to crack now that his tongue was too dry to lick them. Still he persevered and stumbled onwards. The dunes had become smaller now and should have been easier to climb, but his energy had left him and it was all he could do to keep upright when advancing. For some reason unknown to him his balance was affected and at times he could have sworn that the sand hills moved instead of himself. Some sort of illusion, he supposed. Perhaps he was going just a little mad in the way that Oakley had once described before an enthralled after-dinner audience.

His neck burned with sharp stabs of pain. There was nothing he could do about it. If he tore off the sleeve of the thin army shirt and used it to shield his neck like a sort of scarf, then the upper parts of his arms would soon begin to suffer. He was too exhausted to shield the sun-burnt skin anyway. A kind of apathy about his situation had now developed. Presently he would die if no help came, but the thought itself gave him no terror. Onwards he staggered whilst the fiery furnace of the sun above glared malevolently down upon him.

An hour later he groped his way weakly over the blistering slip-face of a dune and met Thompson. The sergeant was standing there at the base of the hillock, his friendly, fat face smiling in welcome, a water bottle in his hand.

'Thank God,' croaked Taylor, his blackened lips splitting with the effort of speaking, 'you've found me at last.' He stumbled and fell, rolling down the slope towards the burly figure of the soldier, and blackness descended as he passed out unconscious.

When he came to he was still in the same spot, the sun beating and scorching upon his back. He lifted his head slowly. The sand in front of him was undisturbed. No Sergeant Thompson was there. There never had been. Despair gripped him in its cruel talons. Much later, as if like an automaton, his tortured body shuffled forward, but why it did so he could not say.

Ginah sat still and silent, her eyes and expression vacant. For the moment she was but an instrument by which her mistress probed the uncertain future. Only one of the many visions seen reflected in the girl's eyes would be the correct version, but it was possible for a highly trained observer to eliminate many of the less likely possibilities. Now there was one particular scene which claimed the watcher's attention. Somewhere further away than time itself, the diminutive figure of a man struggled against the desert, like an insect crawling on a dusty road.

'Yes, ant-man, crawl on,' she whispered softly, 'you may yet succeed where others have failed before you.' She woke Ginah from the trance and having sent the girl away, retired for the night.

CHAPTER TWELVE

The attack came without warning an hour before dawn. Ginah rushed into their room and awoke them hastily, telling them the bad news that Zaduk and Tokin's forces had entered the castle at one point and were even now advancing inwards. Her Lady Serainis had given instructions to awake and bring them to her apartments on the east side of the castle. They dressed quickly and hurried through the large, long corridors, past numerous armed men preparing for battle. Ginah took them through an anteroom and up a short flight of stairs to a small private room where Serainis was, dressed in a travelling costume of white fur, with long boots made from tough leather.

'Shut the door, Ginah, and throw the bolt across to prevent entry from the other side.'

Ginah's slight form wrestled with the heavy iron bar until Jeron came to her aid and gained an unnoticed look of thanks from her. He guessed that the speaker was Syndra, for her sister would conserve her available energy whenever possible due to her extreme weakness.

'My friends, this is not a council-of-war, for the purpose of such is to take decisions regarding possible courses of action, and in this case my divinations clearly show that the battle is lost.'

There was a startled cry from Yola. 'Then we are also lost,' she exclaimed, 'for the enemy does not keep prisoners alive for long. What can we do faced with such a fate?'

A cold smile of amusement played momentarily on the lovely face of Serainis. 'There is no need to panic, girl. We are not yet taken, nor have I any such intention of allowing us to be. We will shortly leave this castle forever by a route unknown to the enemy or indeed even by my closest admirers, whose services I have enlisted to cover our retreat.'

The meaning of her words slowly dawned upon Jeron, who was appalled at her callousness. 'What, do you mean us to flee from this place while your soldiers still fight on in your name and their women folk are being caught and ravished by the enemy? Does their commander retreat whilst the troops still fight? What manner of custom is this?'

Syndra turned towards him and he wilted under the intense look from those electrifying eyes of hers.

'Fool,' she hissed, 'do you think that I spend good lives easily and allow pain with dishonour to take the place of beauty and goodness? Still I forgive you for your remarks for even yet you know me not. What is written in the future nobody can read with surety, but a few such as myself, can see but a part of the truth revealed by sorcery. The people that die today are those condemned by Fate in any case. They have no reprieve. With us it is different, for we may shape our own deliverance. You have much to learn, Jeron, and in being favoured to act as my travelling companion would best be prepared to listen well, speaking only with constructive suggestions.'

She checked that their clothing was adequate and gave Yola a thicker coat to wear. Ginah gave them each provisions for what appeared to be a long journey ahead. Syndra opened the door of a cupboard to reveal a small armoury, from which she selected some weapons. They each received a bow and a quiver of metal-tipped arrows. Jeron also chose a longer sword than the one he had been carrying. From below them a sound of steps came quickly up the stairs. The door was tried and a shout of rage greeted them from the other side. More steps came up as further troops arrived.

'Now is the time,' said Syndra, her face alive with excitement almost as if she were enjoying the situation whilst the others were being terrified. 'Join hands so that we are standing in the form of a square.'

Mystified they linked hands, Jeron being next to Syndra and Ginah. A loud crashing was heard on the other side of the door as the troops outside endeavoured to force their way in. Syndra told them to repeat certain words of magic five times, whilst she chanted a stream of words which sounded complete gibberish to Jeron. Suddenly without any warning the whole room began to move circular-wise about them. Round and round the floor beneath them moved, faster and faster, until the separate images of the furniture in the room became fused together in blurred lines of a circular pattern. He heard the shattering crash as the door split open and saw as in a dream part of the pattern alter in a subtle way as the troops rushed in, but there was nobody inside for the soldiers to see.

They flew through space as if their bodies were no weight at all. The strain upon their wrists and arms became almost unbearable. They whirled round at an incredible rate and all the time Syndra the witch chanted her spell to speed them on that fantastic journey. Vague impressions of light and dark came to them but their own forms were the only definite shapes visible. Yola opposite him held her slim body rigid, her white face always seeking his for moral support. Ginah's fingers gripped his arm so tightly that her nails pierced the skin slightly, adding pain to his emotions. She too had fixed her gaze upon him and her face wore a look of contentment as if she drew substantial comfort from the physical contact with him. He turned his head to watch Syndra muttering the cabbalistic message and was alarmed to see an awful change wrought in the beauty of that person. She looked terribly ill, her skin was sallow, her eyes tired. The words that had come easily from her lips now were whispered as her head rolled

144

from side to side as if in agony. Aghast, he felt her hand slipping away from his grip. He pulled with all his effort and held her, but even as he succeeded, Yola lost her other hand and the revolving square was broken. At once they were hurtled through space in an agonising fury of forces beyond their control. Winds rushed screaming past them, wrenching and pulling at their hair and clothes. Downwards they swept into a great black cloud of oblivion that swiftly rose up to meet them. There was a sudden jarring crash and then they knew no more.

Much later he heard a voice calling to him. 'Jeron, Jeron, wake up.' His name was called again by Ginah who was bending over him, his head cradled in her arms. He groaned as feeling returned and swept through his bruised body, awakening the nerves. He opened his eyes. A blue sky greeted him. It was very cold. Huge trees were on all sides and carried traces of snow on their branches. Ginah spoke to him again with wonder in her voice.

'Ah, now you are at last awake and my dreams have been realised. Neither the one nor the other shall have you now, for we alone have survived this ordeal. Serainis is dead, which in a way is a pity though I do not regret her passing, for though there were bonds between us, yet not one was of love itself. It is a pity about your Yola and no doubt you will mourn her for some while to come, though in the end I shall still be with you when her name slips completely from your memory.' She bent over him and kissed him tenderly on the lips, but as she did so, a cry came from a few yards further off, and Yola began to stir on the frosty ground. Jeron gently disengaged himself from Ginah's embrace and got to his feet, still somewhat dazed. They went over to Yola and helped her to sit up, Ginah biting her lip in vexation that her rival was still alive, although pleased also for Yola's sake, since the girl had never borne her any malice or indeed had any apparent reason to do so. Yola looked drunkenly around her and laughed a little hysterically. 'Where is the great sorceress who dropped us in mid-flight?'

Ginah pointed to a still figure on the ground some distance away. When they got nearer they could see that she was not dead as Ginah had thought, but nevertheless was very ill indeed. Jeron guessed that the efforts induced by Syndra to make the spell work had been too much for the already weak Serainis, whose physical collapse had affected the recent course of events.

'Syndra,' he said, 'can you hear me? We are still here with you. How can we help?'

The voice came faintly in reply. 'Alas, this time you cannot aid me. Serainis is dying and thus too am I, for when this body and her soul is dead as you would describe it, my spirit will leave it also. Then you will know us no more. Ginah, give me the flask of essence of Thyros which is kept in the box of potions, for I would defer the arrival of Death for a while.'

Ginah produced a small bottle of fluorescent green liquid and helped her mistress to swallow a small quantity of this. Then the ailing woman sank back and motioned the onlookers away. 'Leave me now, for Serainis and I would die in peace, alone, but with each other, as when we first set eyes upon this sorry world.'

They made her more comfortable and then they left her there to commune amongst each other some way further off.

'This is terrible. Is there nothing we can do?' asked Yola, looking from one to the other.

Ginah shook her head. 'The only hope is if we can keep Serainis and Syndra alive together but it seems that this malady of Serainis needs greater and more powerful healing than we could ever give.'

'Wait a moment,' exclaimed Jeron excitedly, 'I still have the ring.' He explained to Ginah some of the properties of the device. 'Do you remember how its power once healed an injury received by you, Yola, when your horse had thrown you to the ground? Perhaps it will help Serainis to recover if I direct the power to her. We have nothing else to offer so let's use it if Syndra has no objections.'

He explained his proposal to Syndra who examined the ring with great interest for a few moments, but then fell back exhausted with the effort of maintaining the body of Serainis upright. She nodded in agreement and so he began to draw on the power of the ring, feeding it in turn to her body. The band of metal grew warmer as more intense power was directed to the sick woman lying on the ground before him. Soon her body began to scintillate with an eerie blue light as she absorbed even greater quantities of the life-giving energy. Jeron's finger began to burn as the heat from the metal became even greater. He removed the ring and placed it on one of the fingers of Serainis. He backed rapidly away as the aura of light surrounding her grew so bright that it dazzled his eyes. The air began to crackle and long, silver sparks flew through the air. From the inert body a stream of light flowed and once again he saw the two astral bodies of the spirits hovering over the body. As the three of them looked on at this amazing sight, the diminutive shape of Serainis's spirit gradually increased in size, whilst that of Syndra's diminished until the two ghost-like forms became equal in size. Then the aura around the body leapt up and filled the two visions with its strange light, and as it did so the two became one as they melted into each other and reformed as a single, opaque form. This glowed and scintillated with light before it collapsed and poured rapidly back into the woman's body below.

'Whatever does this mean?' demanded Yola in tones of awe and wonder. 'Has Serainis died?'

Ginah put her arm around the other girl's shoulders. 'Yes and no I think,' she said softly, 'both answers being correct in

147

part. I am not sure of course but I think that what has happened is that Serainis has died and been re-born in some mystical way. Now no longer the separate spirits of the twins inhabit her body. Probably what we have seen was the joining together of their spirits. Thus no longer will they be separate identities striving to support each other in surroundings meant only for one. Now they are united completely, for their souls have combined under the strange catalytic effect of the ring. The spirit that motivates this perfect body now is neither Serainis nor Syndra, but a new identity whose character arises from the fusing together of their twin souls. We must help her to orientate herself when she awakes. No longer can we address her as Syndra or Serainis for now neither is a true description.'

Yola gazed at the still figure now sleeping deeply. 'What then shall we call her who is thus reborn not as an infant but as a fully grown woman?'

Jeron smiled at that question from his beloved Yola. 'I am sure that she will tell us her new name in her own time. If her new personality is like that of the twins then I would hesitate to interfere too much. As it is she may not thank me for the changes effected by the ring.'

'No, I am sure you are wrong there. Serainis would not have lived much longer in the poor state that she was in. Besides, did not Syndra agree to the idea of using the power provided by the ring?'

They continued chatting about the transformation and waited for their charge to awake. However, the deep sleep continued and they judged it best not to awaken her. The girls set about preparing a simple meal from the provisions they carried, whilst Jeron scanned about him for some dry wood to make a fire. The place seemed very desolate. When he had picked up enough wood he turned around to rejoin the girls and nearly jumped out of his skin with fright. A pace away from him stood an old man with a huge dome of a forehead and very piercing eyes, who regarded him with an uncomfortably critical stare. He wore a long robe of gold-coloured material and supported himself with a stout wooden stick. Almost like some carved ivory figure, he gazed back at Jeron with an intensity hard to counter. The girls seemed to be unaware of his presence and continued their chatting further off.

'My pardon,' said Jeron nervously, 'I did not see you there a moment ago.'

The old man half smiled. 'It is not surprising; you were not looking for me. However, I in turn have looked for you. It seems that your work is finally ended.' He pointed with his stick to the body of the sleeping woman that once had been Serainis and chuckled. Jeron felt an icy chill up his spine as he suddenly saw that the old man cast no shadow on the ground.

'Are you the one who sent me on this mission, the great seer Pandilex himself, that died many years ago?'

The piercing eyes regarded the young man without emotion. 'I am just a shade, a mere memory of what was once a man of all knowledge. Compared with him I am but a wisp of smoke from the great fire that once roared forth. No man may conquer Death, the invincible warrior, though a few may forestall its final victory for a time. Cease to wonder who or what I am, for the answer may not be given. It is sufficient to know that you have accomplished the purpose of your task, directed as it was by the will of Pandilex, for by your actions you have discovered the reasons why Serainis failed to return to her father in his lifetime. You have shown that her intentions, as always in the past, have been entirely noble. Unfortunately the malign spirit of Syndra also inhabited the body of her sister and thus influenced the evil course of events which led to the deaths of Tiros and his soldiers, and the attempts upon the lives of yourself and your companion. Despite the ready excuses given for these deeds, the fact remains that whilst

Serainis's spirit withered and weakened, that of Syndra grew bloated, sucking as a leech on the substance of her sister's soul. This monstrosity left to its own devices would have fed upon Serainis until that pure soul would have been totally lost forever. Therefore the evil of Syndra's soul has been finally and totally annihilated by the last act of dead Pandilex. Now like a tree from which a blighted bough has been cut off, Serainis the pure will live again in all her loveliness and goodness.

'Yet your task is not completely finished, for one last thing remains for you to do. It is necessary that for a time Serainis must remain in a state of suspended animation whilst regenerative life processes act within her ailing system. Only after a specified period will her body be strong enough to support life as you define it, for she has received a terrible shock upon the destruction of her sister's soul. So great has been this shock that the healing process would normally take decades of years before awakening could occur with impunity to her health. However, it is known that far away there exist other planets and suns where the laws that govern orderly synchronisation of time no longer hold true. Travel between such worlds and this globe of ours is sometimes possible, but can take place in one way only for obvious reasons. You, Jeron, came from such a planet upon the request of Pandilex. You can never return there, for once lost you cannot regain the correct phase in time, time being an irreversible quantity. Here you must settle down and live out your years, enjoying life in the best way of which you are capable.

'Serainis will travel back along a similar path to the one that you once took; because the secrets of the routes to these far-off worlds are closely guarded, even Pandilex only knew with any certainty of one such way, being the route to your world. She will go there, never to return, but safe from the ravages of time during the healing process, for unlike yourself, on that far-off planet, she will age so slowly as to be virtually immortal. Thus it is that Serainis, the one good daughter of the greatest magician of all time, will receive her inheritance and be as a Goddess upon your planet.

'You will therefore carry out certain preparations in order that she may be sent to a particular place of safety on your world, where during the healing period her body will be immune from all outside dangers. One day, when the time is right, a catalyst will awake her from the protecting coma of sleep and she will claim her rightful inheritance.

'When she has finally gone from this present point in our cosmic system your part in all this will have ceased. Then be advised by me and travel westwards over the grey mountains, for in that direction lies a city of great fortune, wherein you will find a home to live in and much happiness. Now I return whence I came, for soon shall the spirit of Pandilex sleep at last in the dream of Eternity.' So saying, he vanished.

Jeron walked back to the girls and explained what had happened. It was ironic that Serainis would be going to the very place desired by Syndra. However, as Yola said, this situation was different now, for Pandilex had destroyed the evil that was Syndra, and the good character of Serainis had been proved to the complete satisfaction of her father. It seemed after all that their interpretation of the phenomena caused by the ring was wrong, for one of the spirits had been destroyed by the will of Pandilex. The girls listened intently to his story and the details of the instructions regarding Serainis. They decided to wait until next morning before journeying on, for the light was already beginning to fade amongst the tall fir trees.

They set up two skin tents, one for Yola and Jeron, and the other for Serainis and Ginah. The latter seemed content to tend Serainis and so the others left her to it. Soon the fire burnt down and all was quiet. The meal that Ginah had prepared with Yola had caused them all to feel very drowsy and they all slept deeply that night. Jeron dreamed of Serainis as he slept and imagined that she came into the tent naked and beautiful as always, to lie down between Yola and himself. It was only a dream he knew in a vague sort of way, but the sleeping presence of Yola made the whole thing seem wrong somehow. He struggled to awake, to open his eyes properly, but he was bound within the fantasy and as the nude with the glittering eyes made love to him his resistance weakened and he allowed her to have her way with him. Later he slept more deeply, and this time there were no erotic dreams.

The next day they set out according to the directions given by Jeron's vision. He carried the inert body in his arms and marvelled at Serainis's beauty as she slept in the trance. Her angelic attractiveness was even more pronounced now that the undesirable influence of Syndra had been removed. They left the clearing where they had arrived and walked along a natural pathway that inclined sharply downwards. Much later on they came across a large cave. Once this had been inhabited but now no one lived there. In front of the entrance lay the path of a huge glacier in which were embedded numerous rocks and stones of all sizes. The warmth of the suns above did not penetrate the surface of the ice and a thick frost lay underfoot on the spiky grass. Jeron searched as he had been directed for a part of the ice river which was clear and free of particles. Eventually he selected a spot where the ice was like crystal and he could see well into the depths below. When he touched the glacier he found it was surprisingly much colder than he had estimated. Certainly the hoar frost on the grass felt warm by comparison and he wondered why the temperature of the glacier kept so low. Another mystery in this world of the unusual.

They carried her with some difficulty on to the slippery surface of the glacier and laid her down on the ice. When they clambered back to the bank, they found that where their hands had touched the ice, there were red blisters forming, just as if they had been burnt. Serainis slept on the ice, her face turned upwards towards the sky. Contact with the glacier did not produce the same burns that the others had suffered from. As they watched her, the ice around the body slowly melted and re-froze over, as she gradually sank below the surface. When she was a few feet below the glassy surface her descent slowed and Jeron scratched with a knife a large rectangle upon the ice above her. Then certain signs were written on to this and when the task was completed Jeron looked critically at his handiwork to check that he had written all the runes that the vision had shown to him. They waited to see what would happen and at first could detect nothing at all out of the ordinary. The misty figure inside the glacier lay corpse-like but somewhere within they knew that life was flickering even yet, not dead but dormant.

Yola pointed to the ice. 'See, something is happening. The ice around the rectangle is melting fast.'

'Yes,' said Ginah excitedly, 'the top surface of it is now protruding above the rest of the river. Either the block of ice is rising or floating upwards, or the river height is decreasing.'

The latter possibility proved to be correct for as time went on the glacier ice around the block melted and flowed away down the mountain-side. Towards evening however the glacier began to freeze again and eventually the surface was as before although the glacier was much lower now, and the great hexagonal block of ice containing Serainis lay on top of the lowered surface.

Again Jeron carved runes on the four upright sides of the block. Last of all he wrote in deep letters on the ice the name Serainis. Then he stepped back and slipped on the ice, half-falling backwards. He steadied himself and rejoined the others.

Somewhere in the air above them a voice spoke and words of power were uttered. There was a terrible, blinding flash before their eyes and a great pressure of air around them. In that instant, as they later discovered when they talked about it, they all received the same vivid impression in their minds of an immense green rock below which was a cave. Over the entrance to this were written the same runes that Jeron had himself carved upon the block. The picture faded as quickly as it had come and the three companions then saw that the block of ice was no longer before them. They stood there in silence, awed by the suddenness and power of the event.

Later they got ready for the long journey that lay ahead of them. Whilst Ginah checked their supplies, Yola walked over to where Jeron was. She slipped her arm about his waist and looked up at his thoughtful face.

'What are you so pensive about?' she asked him with a gentle smile.

He looked down at her and smiled back. 'I wonder where she is now. Will we ever see her again or is she indeed lost forever to this planet?'

Yola looked about her at the numerous constellations in the sky, gradually fading as the morning sun began to rise. 'Some day she will awake as has been foretold, but when that day will come no one can predict. Who knows, we may yet meet again.'

Ginah came up to them. 'We are ready now. All has been checked.'

'Right then,' said Jeron, 'let us depart. We have a long journey in front of us, but if the vision was correct our future happiness lies at our destination.' He turned to go, but Yola gently caught his arm. She looked up at his strong, bronzed face with a strange light in her eyes .

'Don't you mind,' she asked softly, 'that you will never see your world again?'

He thought for a little while and then shook his head. 'No,' he replied firmly, 'I shall not miss what I do not remember.

Besides this planet is my world now, and home will always be where my sweet Yola is.' He smiled broadly and then kissed her.

They began the final journey home. Ginah followed them a little way behind. She watched them and smiled a little. They would have their happiness but she would also have hers. Inside the oval ebony box which she carried with her were a number of beautiful life-like masks and some phials of a certain deep blue liquid which once had belonged to her mistress. On certain nights when Yola slept more deeply than usual, Ginah, the unwanted, would visit the dreams of Jeron and live again the night of all nights.

CHAPTER THIRTEEN

The glare of light all around him was terrible. Now he had lost all sense of direction although his blistered feet still tottered on. Somewhere the dunes had been left behind and the ground was firmer now. He fell over something hard and crashed to the ground. Dimly he realised that the obstacle was a rock. He stretched forth his shaking hands and felt it hard and unyielding. There were others about on the ground and he knew then that the desert had ended. This was somewhere on the edge where the scrubland started. He put his hands over his eyes and tried to make out the surroundings. Ahead of him something large and dark loomed up. His legs felt paralysed since he had stopped walking and so he began to slowly crawl towards what he had seen.

It was only a few yards away, but it took him an hour to reach its shadow. The relief from the heat was indescribable. Even the dark green rock about him felt cool and welcoming. He recovered enough to realise that he was at the entrance to a large cave. There were carvings on the rock to prove that others had been here too at some distant time, but he was in no state to admire the archeology. He dragged his body into the cave and discovered a miracle. The floor was covered in water.

He drank painfully and pressed his tortured body against the sodden ground. Relief greeted him as he lost consciousness, his body outstretched and arms extended before him. Water dripped down at his side while he slept.

Several hours later he awoke and drank thirstily from the pool of water beneath his face. Then he sat up and looked around him. There was nothing, absolutely nothing to see. He was blind, perhaps only temporarily, but nevertheless without that vital sense. This came as a great shock to him and he panicked until reason set into his mind the thought that here he could exist for several days, until the army came and found him. There was certainly enough water to drink. He stood up with an effort and began to cautiously feel his surroundings. He was obviously in a large natural cave, although the source of the water was a mystery. There was little to do apart from rest, and after a few hours he decided to track down the source of the water. By walking carefully in various directions and listening to the sound of dripping water, he discovered that the noise was coming from an inner chamber.

There was a gap large enough for him to squeeze through and he entered this with some caution after receiving a couple of vicious blows to the head from projecting overhead rocks. He approached the centre of this cave from where the water was dripping and advanced slowly, testing the ground in front in case he inadvertently fell into some underground pool. His hands made contact with something extremely cold and slippery. A piece broke off in his grasp and melted away. It was ice. Incredulously he felt around it. A massive block of ice lay before him, some six feet high and as long.

Nothing of this made any sense to him. How could this immense iceberg have originated in such surroundings and why was most of it still in solid form? The shape of it was too regular to have evolved naturally in any case. He sat down and hastily got up again. The water was extremely cold. There was nothing else of interest, so he returned to the main cavern.

After two days his sight began to return and he could dimly observe objects as if through a thick haze. The iceberg he now saw was as he had imagined it to be from his sense of touch. The interior was darker as if something were trapped inside the centre part, but it took him another day for his sight to improve still further before he began to have suspicions about the contents.

As the ice melted so the block diminished in size and he was able to see inside with great clarity. What he saw was the body of a young woman stretched out within the ice. Although his initial feelings were of horror and disgust, they gave way to a curious feeling of interest as he gradually saw how lovely was the face of the girl. The mystery of the ice block and how it had come to be here, combined with the beauty of the corpse, intrigued him so much that he forgot the hours passing by, as he waited for the rescue party which he hoped would come.

It occurred to him that soon the body would be freed of its icy prison and that exposure to the warm air would then affect its perfect state of preservation. Within a few hours then the corpse would become an unwelcome silent inhabitant of his haven. He decided that when the time came he would have to take it outside the cave and bury it. At least she would have that much done for her. If no rescue party came for him, he would have no such burial.

The last vestiges of ice melted away and she lay there, cold and beautiful, perfect even in death. He decided to carry her into the outer cave so that he could observe her in the better light before he buried her. She was light and no effort to carry. He put her down reverently at the mouth of the cave where the rays from the evening sun warmed her skin.

He sat there humbly beside her and gazed at the perfect features of that saintly face. She might have been an angel for all he knew. If she had been alive he would have worshipped her, for no woman he had ever seen possessed such divine beauty as this. An hour passed and still he lingered at that hallowed resting-place. The skin was warmer now and he could almost believe that she was alive, just sleeping there, although he knew in his heart of hearts that she was utterly dead.

A movement in the desert caught his eye and he looked up. There it was again, a tiny army lorry in the distance, weaving in and out of the dunes. He stood up and went to the cave entrance to signal his presence, but at the last moment something indefinable made him hesitate. There was a prickling feeling at the back of his scalp. Slowly he turned around. Surely those eyelids had been closed before! Glittering green eyes stared wide open back at him. Terrified but fascinated, he turned and walked slowly towards the corpse. Taylor knelt down and stared into those glinting, unmoving eyes which absorbed his complete attention. Had there ever been a creature more beautiful than this? On an impulse he took the lovely face in his hands, brushed aside the long, damp hair and kissed those ice-cold lips. Ever-widening pools of emerald green enveloped his mind as her pretty white hands fluttered up and delicately rested on either side of his thin, sun-burnt neck. They began to squeeze harder and harder. He struggled in vain to stare away from that lovely face of goodness and purity. Taylor's face became blue as his chest heaved with the effort to force air into his lungs. The last things he saw as blackness engulfed him and he collapsed dead before her were those paralysing, inhuman, emerald eyes.

As the body became limp and dropped heavily to the sand, something hardly visible to a normal person exuded from the corpse and hovered for an instant like a wisp of smoke in the warm, dry air. The cold ruby lips reached forward and sucked it swiftly in. The half-angel smiled. She didn't need her sister now.

All Sphere Books are available at your bookshop or
newsagent, or can be ordered from the following address:
Sphere Books, Cash Sales Department,
P.O. Box 11, Falmouth, Cornwall.

Please send cheque or postal order (no currency), and allow
18p for the first book plus 8p per copy for each additional
book ordered up to a maximum charge of 66p in U.K.

Customers in Eire and B.F.P.O. please allow 18p for the first
book plus 8p per copy for the next 6 books, thereafter 3p
per book.

Overseas customers please allow 20p for the first book and
10p per copy for each additional book.